The Last Word

With Longarm's pistol still pressed against his ear, Duncan Swords had his hands raised, looking for all the world like a carved Italian-marble statue. Longarm leaned down in Swords's face almost nose-to-nose.

"Remember what I just said, and what you just saw, Swords. You and your boys best toe the line while you're in Tascosa—as long as I'm here. Otherwise, I'll throw all three of you in jail and forget about you. Now nod, like I've actually made myself as clear as a barrel of fresh rainwater." Swords's fingers twitched, but his head bobbed once . . .

TABOR EVANS

LONGARM

AND THE TASCOSA TWO-STEP

J

JOVE BOOKS, NEW YORK

THE BERKLEY PUBLISHING GROUP
Published by the Penguin Group
Penguin Group (USA) Inc.
375 Hudson Street, New York, New York 10014, USA
Penguin Group (Canada), 90 Eglinton Avenue East, Suite 700, Toronto, Ontario M4P 2Y3, Canada
(a division of Pearson Penguin Canada Inc.)
Penguin Books Ltd., 80 Strand, London WC2R 0RL, England
Penguin Group Ireland, 25 St. Stephen's Green, Dublin 2, Ireland (a division of Penguin Books Ltd.)
Penguin Group (Australia), 250 Camberwell Road, Camberwell, Victoria 3124, Australia
(a division of Pearson Australia Group Pty. Ltd.)
Penguin Books India Pvt. Ltd., 11 Community Centre, Panchsheel Park, New Delhi—110 017, India
Penguin Group (NZ), 67 Apollo Drive, Mairangi Bay, Auckland 1310, New Zealand
(a division of Pearson New Zealand Ltd.)
Penguin Books (South Africa) (Pty.) Ltd., 24 Sturdee Avenue, Rosebank, Johannesburg 2196,
South Africa

Penguin Books Ltd., Registered Offices: 80 Strand, London WC2R 0RL, England

This is a work of fiction. Names, characters, places, and incidents either are the product of the author's imagination or are used fictitiously, and any resemblance to actual persons, living or dead, business establishments, events, or locales is entirely coincidental.

LONGARM AND THE TASCOSA TWO-STEP

A Jove Book / published by arrangement with the author

PRINTING HISTORY
Jove edition / February 2007

ISBN: 978-0-515-14254-9

JOVE®
Jove Books are published by The Berkley Publishing Group,
a division of Penguin Group (USA) Inc.,
375 Hudson Street, New York, New York 10014.
JOVE is a registered trademark of Penguin Group (USA) Inc.
The "J" design is a trademark belonging to Penguin Group (USA) Inc.

PRINTED IN THE UNITED STATES OF AMERICA

10 9 8 7 6 5 4 3 2 1

Chapter 1

A roiling, gunmetal-gray thundercloud of tobacco smoke swirled around Marshal Billy Vail's rapidly balding, wispy-haired head. He slid backward into the lumpy cushion of his creaking office chair, puffed on an ax-handle-sized cigar clenched between yellow-stained teeth, and stared at Custis Long in stunned disbelief. "Whaddaya mean, 'nope'? You're not even going to argue with me this time? Hell, I thought sure you'd get your stinger out, like one of those bright orange Mexican hornets, and put bumps all over my head the way you usually do. Jeez, can't believe I've gone and got myself all heated up for one helluva hot dance that ain't even gonna take place. If you want my personal opinion, though, whole damned affair don't seem like much more'n a paid vacation." Long offered no response. "Talkin' to me today, or are you just gonna sit there and grin at me like a shit-eatin' dog?"

Across the paper-littered expanse of Vail's overburdened, and much abused, mahogany desk, Deputy U.S. Marshal Long pulled himself up in the tack-decorated, Moroccan-leather seat. He shot his boss a toothy smile.

1

"Not today, Billy." Vail slapped his desk with the palm of a soft, pink hand, and feigned shocked surprise.

Longarm languidly drew a nickel cheroot from between chapped lips and, once again, flashed an expanse of polished, pearly choppers. "Swear 'fore Jesus it ain't no problem, Billy. Honest to God, I truly like the whole idea of goin' on down to Tascosa. Damned nice little town. Since most of the cattle drives comin' from South Texas on their way up to Dodge have slowed to a trickle, it's a right pleasant place to visit and relax a bit." He burrowed back into the overstuffed comfort of the chair and added, "'Sides, got friends I haven't seen in a spell that live out that way. Female friends, if'n you get my drift."

Vail shook his head and mumbled a plaintive, "Jesus." Then Long's boss bent forward, folded his arms, and rested them on top of the beleaguered desk. He chewed the enormous, smoldering, half-smoked stogie on one side of his mouth then the other. "Well, as I've previously intimated, this assignment shouldn't be any chore a'tall for a big doer like you, Longarm."

"Yeah, well, I heard you say it. And I'm gonna trust you, this time. But you know, Billy, therein lies the pointy nub of an irritating problem. Just exactly what does this particular *mission* involve? Come on, gimme the whole animal—teeth, hair, eyeballs, toenails, and all."

Vail's glance darted around the office. He took note of the loud ticking from the banjo-shaped clock on the wall behind his favorite deputy, then, for a moment, busied himself with a less-than-casual restacking of several piles of Wanted posters and other official-looking federal government documents. Finally, and with great ceremony, he fished a single sheet from one of the teetering stacks, pushed all the other busywork aside, and, once again, locked eyes with Longarm. "All you've gotta do," he said from behind a winning smile, "is mosey on down that way and report to Judge Henry Cain. That fine, upstanding, Amarillo-based adjudicator has formally requested the U.S. marshal's service provide him with protection before, during, and for a few weeks after an upcoming trial."

"When does this *upcoming* trial commence?"

"Supposed to start a week from tomorrow." Vail waved the page in the smiling face of his deputy, dropped it, and watched as the single sheet floated to the edge of the desk.

Longarm scooped the document up and placed it in his brown-tweed lap with little more than a cursory glance. He picked a dangling sprig of loose tobacco from the tip of his nickel cheroot and absentmindedly flicked it onto the dusty carpet beside his chair. "What the hell's goin' on with Judge Cain that he feels the need to send for our help? Can't his court-appointed bailiffs, or the Tascosa city marshal, or maybe the Oldham County sheriff's law-dogs provide him with all necessary safeguards?"

"Not ours to question his motives, or needs. If any judge within our jurisdiction asks for it, we render un-qualified aid, as you well know. But, as nearly as I've been able to ascertain from his letter, the courts down in Amarillo have saddled him with a change-of-venue case that has the man worried for his future health and well-being. Seems he's been getting notes and letters threaten-ing bodily harm and bloody murder ever since the case got sent his direction. And he feels, as do I, that the weighty presence of a deputy U.S. marshal will have con-siderable more impact than any available town or country law on nipping such threats in the bud."

Longarm glanced at the letter again without reading any of it, then pitched the page back on top of Billy Vail's accumulated mess. "That a fact?" A fleeting vision of the naked, heaving, full-breasted body of Rosarita Hernandez, just one of his female "acquaintances" in Tascosa, uncontrollably flashed across the backs of his eyeballs, and he smiled once again. Ah, Rosarita, he thought. 'Course if Rosarita ain't available there's always Consuelo Gonzalez—the hottest living female in North Texas. As he now fondly remembered, sticking his prong into Consuelo was the rough equivalent of trying to hump a bucking bed of hot lava.

"Indeed, yes indeed, it is. For my part, I can completely understand the concern expressed in Judge Cain's missive."

"Why's that, Billy? What, exactly, have you not yet told me? Be thorough, now. Don't hold anything back. You know I hate surprises."

Vail tapped a twitching finger against the pocket of his vest, jerked a fist-sized gold-plated ticker out, glanced at the time, then shoved it back into its hiding place. "Well, the threats could have some considerable weight." His eyebrows knitted with concern. "Seems the killer sent up to Tascosa from Amarillo is none other than Bronson Tull—firstborn son of Rufus Tull."

In an instant, all the fog-laden cobwebs that had covered Custis Long's brain—the result of the previous night's drunken debauchery—were swept away. He ran a hand under one side of his hat and scratched his head. "Rufus Tull's son, huh? Damn, Billy, ain't no doubt, then. Judge Cain could have his hands full."

"Well, that's precisely why he asked for my *best* man."

Longarm knitted his thick eyebrows into lightning

4

bolts and shot Vail a less than trusting look. "Oh, you don't say? Asked for your *best* man, did he?"

"Absolutely." Vail shook a knotted finger at the discarded letter. "If you had bothered to read that," he said, "you'd have noted that he specifically requested the one and only Deputy U.S. Marshal Custis Long, and none other."

"Well, now, I'm just flattered all to hell and gone, but there's four or five of them damned Tull brothers, if memory serves. Seems like I remember an especially bad one named Hogart."

"Nope. Nope. Don't have to do any worryin' 'bout that son of a bitch. Month or so ago, the man got hisself rudely murdered by a woman of questionable virtue."

"Damnation, Billy, now that's what I'd call great news. Must admit I hadn't heard a thing about the evil skunk's fortunate passage to the netherworld. Where'd the lady manage to rid decent society of his sorry presence?"

"Hell's Half Acre, down in Fort Worth. Seems he got earth-shakingly drunk, raped her in the most brutal fashion imaginable, then proceeded to beat the unmerciful hell out of her. Reports, forwarded to me from local law enforcement, have it that he'd done as much to several other women in the same parlor house before. But this last time around, he applied the typical Tull 'treatment' to the wrong soiled dove."

Longarm shook his head and angrily spat, "Any man as would beat a woman deserves whatever he gets, Billy."

"Well, Hogart evidently got his—in spades. Way I heard the ugly tale, the badly battered demimonde finally took all of his brutal attention she could stand, pulled one of those Colt .41-caliber Clover-Leaf house pistols that women favor from under her mattress, popped him twice right betwixt his beady, ratlike little eyes, then shot his nuts off."

Longarm stomped his foot, slapped a knee, and snorted, "Good for her. Damned good shootin'."

"I agree. Knocked him back on his heels and blew most of his brains onto the ceiling and wall, according to Fort Worth's city marshal. Man says ole Hogart was on the way to being dead before he hit the floor, but he must've flopped around a bit, 'cause he slung blood all over hell and yonder, as he finally passed on over to the care and kind attentions of Satan."

"Well, by God, I'm glad to hear it. But, be that as it may, sons of bitches like Hogart Tull always have brothers, or cousins, or uncles, or some other wad of half-witted relatives. Seems like I remember the worst of the bunch was one named Seth. Another called Danko. Way most folks from down that way tell it, Danko's almost as bad as Seth, but not quite."

Vail pulled the cigar from his mouth and thumped a two-inch chunk of gray ash into an overflowing bowl. "Danko might well've been so mean his mother had to feed him with a slingshot. But, thanks be to a benevolent God, he went and got his bad self lynched over in Ruidoso, New Mexico Territory, a few weeks back."

"Lynched?"

"Yep. Seems some of the fine citizens over that way don't take much to Texas gunmen comin' to town and tryin' to steal from their banks."

"So that leaves Seth, the old man, and maybe, one or two others we don't know about. But shit, Billy, sounds to me like if we were to just sit around and wait long enough the whole sorry-assed, woman-beatin' family might well end up shot or hanged, or maybe stabbed, dragged to death, or something else just as wonderfully brutal."

When Vail smacked the top of the desk with the palm

of his hand it sounded like a pistol shot. "Lord, let it be so," he yelped, then pitched a packet of letters of introduction and travel documents into Longarm's lap. "But in the meantime, you need to get on down to the depot tomorrow mornin', catch the Denver and Rio Grande to Trinidad, where you can connect with the Denver, Texas, and Fort Worth on to Tascosa. Everything you need is in that envelope. Ought to be a right pleasant trip this time of year. Leaves are all turnin', nice sharp nip in the air. Texas panhandle country should prove most agreeable."

Longarm toyed with his travel documents, then picked the envelope up and tapped it against the brim of his hat. "Hang on just a second, Billy. What, exactly, did Bronson Tull do to warrant a change of venue from Amarillo to Tascosa?"

Vail leaned back in his chair. "Almost went the way of his brother Danko. Way I heard it, he got into a scrap in a downtown Amarillo watering hole, shot an unarmed and extremely well-liked man to death right in front of a sizable crowd of witnesses, then just walked away."

"Walked away?"

"Didn't get far. Local constabulary caught him before he could make it out of town. Angry mob of the dead man's closest friends had gathered by then. They swarmed all over the badge toters. Came damned near to stringing ole Bronson up, right on the spot, before the law managed to take control of the situation again. They threw his sorry ass in jail, but realized the potential for a deadly problem. So, now he's sittin' in the Tascosa jail and Judge Henry Cain's gettin' death threats."

Longarm slapped his knee with the envelope several times, then pulled his six-foot-two-inch broad-shouldered and stringy-muscled frame out of the leather nest he'd wallowed out. "Helluva tale, Billy." He waved the package at Vail, tapped it against the brim of his snuff-colored Stetson in salute, turned, then headed for the door.

He took the stone steps outside the Denver Federal Building two at a time, then stopped on the sandstone sidewalk long enough to slip the envelope of travel documents into an inside coat pocket. He flipped up the collar of his suit jacket for protection against the nippy breeze whipping down from the Rocky Mountains fifteen miles to the west. The short walk back to his rooming house would, Longarm hoped, prove pleasant and blessedly uneventful.

Chapter 2

Since he usually kept his possibles bag, saddle, bedroll, and Winchester rifle ready for departure on short notice, Longarm felt no real urgency to get back to his empty rented room. A few blocks from home, he took a short detour and headed over to Larimer Street to stop in at the Holy Moses Saloon. A man could get a full shot of bonded Maryland rye for a decent price at the recently opened watering hole. Purchase of the liquor also entitled him to eat freshly baked bread and mounds of thinly sliced beef from the huge, often replenished platter on the establishment's bar. Such niceties never failed to draw a fresh group of regular, paying, and appreciative customers.

He stepped through the saloon's heavy, spanking-new oak door that framed a piece of fancily etched beveled-glass, and pulled it closed behind him. The room was decorated with dark paneling that was highlighted with subdued but tasteful brass accents, dark leather, and an army of polished cuspidors that stood guard along the foot rail of the bar. An easy, quiet, and contented feeling drew Longarm in like the open arms of a beautiful

9

woman. There existed something about the joint he found welcoming, relaxing, and downright peaceful.

The only other person in the place was a stout, handlebar mustachioed, one-eyed drink slinger named Mike O'Hara. O'Hara waved Longarm in and called out, "Aye, Marshal, it's fine to be seein' ye we are, sir. Be takin' yer favorite seat yonder in the far corner. My distinct pleasure to be bringin' yer favorite beverage and a heapin' helpin' of recently acquired Texas beef and all the fine fixins."

Longarm smiled, touched the brim of his hat, and headed for the comfort and security of the corner table at the far end of a polished mahogany bar topped with a thick slab of veined Italian marble. The brightly mirrored back bar stood three tiers deep in a stunning array of liquors of virtually every kind, color, and description a man could imagine. No question about it, Longarm thought, as he walked by and dragged his finger along the shiny, slick surface. This was, beyond any doubt, the most elegant spot in Denver for a man to stand with his foot on a polished rail and have a beaker of mighty fine gator sweat—for the time being anyway.

He'd barely managed to get seated, when O'Hara bustled up carrying a plate of bread, meat, boiled eggs, and a pickle as thick as a baby's arm in one hand, and a double shot of gold-labeled Maryland rye in the other. The grinning bartender placed everything on the table, stood near Longarm's right hand like a spit-and-polish cavalry orderly on parade and said, "Would ye be needin' anythin' more, Marshal?"

Longarm took a healthy swallow of the rye, surveyed the heaping plate, then said, "Don't think so, Mike.

Looks like you've done me up right fine. Eat all this food, I most certainly won't go to bed hungry tonight."

O'Hara darted a sneaky glance around the empty cantina, then leaned over and almost whispered, "Coulda be speakin' with ye kinda private-like, Marshal?"

Longarm motioned to an empty seat. "What's on your mind, Mike?" he asked as O'Hara pulled the chair away from the table, then repositioned it so the men were nearer to each other. It was the first time Longarm had seen O'Hara that close up, in reasonably good light. The jagged piece of ugly pink flesh that ran from the man's forehead down behind the patch over his damaged eye was clearly evident at such close proximity. The veinlike lump appeared to have been carved with a dull spoon.

O'Hara glanced over his shoulder toward the door, twice, before he leaned even closer still. In a barely audible rasp, he said, "I'm by way of askin' for some advice, Marshal Long. Perhaps even some much needed assistance as well, if ye be a catchin' me drift."

Longarm swallowed a mouthful of his sandwich and washed it down with more of the liquor. He picked at a dangle of stringy beef stuck between his teeth, shot a peek at the offending morsel, flicked it onto the floor, then said, "Well, I'll be most happy to help, if I can, Mike. Forge on. Ask ahead."

The bartender snatched at the towel over his shoulder and twisted it into a knot. "Well, sair, two weeks ago, I'm a thinkin', we started gettin' what can only be tairmed as *troublesome* visits from a gentleman, of what I find it necessary to describe as *questionable* background. He usually comes around on mawrnin's like this, when we've

11

very few, or no customers a'tall. So, in truth, yer appearance here today is kind of fortuitous, in a way."

O'Hara's brogue would probably have been difficult for some folks to understand, but many of Longarm's friends were Irish, and he loved the soft, rounded sounds of their speech. He chewed at another mouthful of the meat and bread concoction, washed it down with more of the rye, then said, "What're you gettin' at when you say *troublesome visits*, Mike?" Sizable cracks in the Holy Moses Saloon's surface tranquility were weaseling their way into Longarm's assessment of the place as he watched the nervous man struggle for the appropriate answer.

Once again, O'Hara cast a nervous glimpse toward the saloon's entrance, as he draped the towel back over his shoulder. He turned to Longarm and pinned him in the seat with a heated glare cast from his one good eye. "This particular gentleman comes a callin' most every day now. Claims to stop in on us by way of sellin' what he calls *insharrance*."

"Insurance?"

A distasteful frown creased the Irishman's brow when he said, "Gent says if the owner ain't by way of boiyin' what he's sellin', our nice, shiny, new place might come to some kind of unknowable calamity."

"Any mention of what kind of calamity?"

"I seem to recall foire, being mentioned a number of toimes."

"Fire? You mean to say, he's threatened to burn the Holy Moses?"

"Not in so many wards, Marshal, but, yes, his message was crystoil clear—the Holy Moses jus' moight go up in flames."

"You expectin' him to stop in for a visit this morning?"

"Would venture to say he probably will. And the owner told me to tell ye as how she would be most grateful if ye'd take a moment to give this fellow a look. Says she'd be interested to find out more about 'im. If that's a'tall possible, doan'cha see."

Longarm had the glass of rye nearly to his lips again. He stopped short and said, "She? The owner of the Holy Moses is a she?"

O'Hara smiled. "Ah, Jazus, tis true, Marshal. Lady of considerable refinement, and a damned good-looker, too. If yer by way of takin' moi meanin'."

The whiskey glass hit the table with a *thump*, and Longarm pushed the snuff-colored Stetson to the back of his head with one finger. "And what might this damned good-looker's name be, Michael, me fine mahn?"

O'Hara's only eye twinkled when he said, "Cora Anne Fisher, Marshal."

"Cora Anne Fisher. Nice name. Like the sound of her already and we've never met."

"You know, Marshal Long, ordinarily I would have already taken care of this situation mine own self. But this fellow ain't the kind to be messin' with, I'm thinkin'. Looks, for all the warld, to be the kind who might've cut his baby teeth on the barrel of a loaded pistol. Perhaps the very one he carries in that shoulder hoilster a hanging under his beefy left arm."

The words had barely passed the jumpy bartender's lips when the front door swung open and hit the wall with a loud *thud*. At almost the same instant, O'Hara's and Longarm's glances darted toward the entry. A muscular, broken-nosed brute, who looked like six feet of coiled rattlesnake dressed in a mouse-gray three-piece suit and derby hat, stepped inside. The burly ruffian had the bear-

13

ing and appearance of a man who intended to clean the place out by beating the proverbial hell out of anyone handy, then taking a blazing hot piss on all those he'd just stomped the bejabbers out of.

O'Hara stood, whipped the towel off his shoulder again, and casually wiped at a spot on Longarm's table. "That's 'im. The vary one, Marshal," he whispered, then heeled it to his server's spot behind the marble-topped counter.

Longarm pushed his unfinished plate of food aside, sipped at his rye, and watched as the "insurance" salesman motioned O'Hara over to the far end of the bar. The two men hovered over a quiet spot close to the entrance. They spoke in subdued, but heated, tones for several minutes. Eventually the discussion became louder and more animated. Then, the alleged "salesman" grabbed a handful of the bartender's apron and shirt, and surprised the hell out of Longarm by slapping O'Hara hard across the face with an open-palmed hand—twice.

Jesus, Longarm thought, I hate to get involved in this. Nothing worse, or stupider, than a bar fight. But when the bruiser slapped O'Hara again, well, that really ripped the rag off the bush.

"That's enough," Longarm shouted, as the third rap in Mike O'Hara's chops still echoed across the room. He pushed his chair away from the table, stood, and stepped to a spot at the bar farthest from the action.

The rattlesnake, muscles so tense he vibrated like a picked banjo string, held on to O'Hara's apron front with a fist the size of a saddlebag. His wide, square head swiveled around on a thick, brutish neck in a tight, rigid semicircle like an iron-bound wagon wheel on an ungreased axle. He blinked at Longarm as if not believing what he'd heard. "This discussion is no concern of your'n, mister," he hissed. "If I 'uz you, I'd be sittin' back down and shuttin' yer stupid fuckin' mouth before someone stuck a booted foot in it all the way down to yer arsehole. Crack that yap of your'n again—just might be forced to come over there and kick your arse so hard you'll have to remove that manure-colored hat to take a shit."

Longarm flipped his coattail back to reveal the silver-plated, bone-gripped, double-action Colt's Frontier model pistol mounted cross-draw fashion on his left side. The bullet-headed viper released his grip on Mike O'Hara's apron and turned to fully face his tormentor, then took two determined, quick steps in Longarm's direction.

"That's far enough, you ugly son of a bitch," Longarm growled and motioned for the bruiser to stop.

Caught short by such an easily and authoritatively delivered command, O'Hara's attacker came to an abrupt halt, swayed like a fully leafed cottonwood in a summer storm, and, for several moments, appeared not to know exactly what he should do. But he quickly recovered and jerked a sausage-sized thumb toward the door. The butt of a .45-caliber English Webley Bulldog peeked out from the shoulder holster under his jacket. "I've had jest about all of yer horseshit I'm likely to take today, mister. Must have a considerable growth of hard bark coverin' yer dumb ass to brace a man like me, while I'm doin' business. Think you'd best hit the street runnin' 'fore I completely run out of patience and whip yer stringy ass like it belongs on a red-headed, ten-year-old stepchild."

Longarm threw his head back and let out a derisive snort. "Take another step in my direction, you big gob of

15

horse slobber," he said, "and there won't be enough of you left to whip a three-year-old, towheaded girl."

The snake made an ever-so-tentative motion like he just might stupidly indulge himself in the forbidden move. Longarm's hand came up to his pistol's comforting grip. "Best give it some serious thought, cocksucker. First thing I'm gonna do, if you make another threatening move, is blow your tiny balls into that spittoon behind you."

Longarm watched as an earthquake of pent-up fury rumbled from the brute's feet all the way to inflamed ears. His neck muscles bulged, and the veins popped out like purple rivers running through a snow-capped mountain of unrelenting anger. "Who the fuck do you think you're a talkin' to like that, mister? You don't know me. And, by God, you can't even begin to imagine how much damage I can do. Get my hands around your scrawny neck and I'll mash your head like a troublesome ass pimple. Render your brains out to nothin' more'n a gob of greasy, gray squzz and skull juice."

Longarm tickled the butt of his pistol again. "It's true enough that I don't know you from a pile of cow shit, mister, but I do know one thing. I'm a deputy U.S. marshal. And if I catch you slinkin' around the Holy Moses again, tryin' to intimidate Mr. O'Hara there, or the owner, customers, or the guy who swamps the floor, or the swamper's three-legged cat for that matter, I'll see to it you spend the next two to four years in the Federal Penitentiary up in Detroit playin' house with No-Thumbs Bucky Matoose. Way I hear it, No-Thumbs Bucky just dearly loves big ole, smart-aleck boys like you."

O'Hara's fearsome attacker bubbled and fumed like an iron kettle filled with hot grease. The sausage-sized

16

fingers twitched, and twice he brought a hand up to the waist of his trousers, only to drop it to his side again. All of a sudden he turned on the heel of a highly polished boot, then stomped his way to the entrance. He grabbed the knob, jerked the door open, then threw a threatening glance over his shoulder. "I'm goin', you badge-wearin' wad of spit. But trust me, I'll be back."

"No you won't," Longarm called out. "See, I'm gonna put out word to every federal officer and policeman in the city limits of Denver that they should be on the lookout for you, and any others like you. There's a bunch of us deputy marshals workin' here out of the First District Court of Colorado. Once word gets around, you won't be able to spit a sprig of tobacco on the sidewalk without one of us knowing. And *you* trust me on this one, mister, should you spit in the wrong place, like the Holy Moses for instance, it's off to Detroit and dancing with No-Thumbs Bucky. My advice is to get out of town now, while you're still walkin' upright and able."

The bullyboy threw Longarm one final, dazzling, hate-filled glance, then shot through the entrance like the flames of hell snapped at his heels. He slammed the door with such force that bottles rattled and danced almost halfway down the back bar.

As Longarm leaned on the Italian-marble slab and lit himself a nickel cheroot, a still shaking Mike O'Hara poured another glass of rye, then hustled down to place the offering in front of his savior.

"Many thanks, sair. Oh, yes, indeed. Oi'm forever in yer debt, Marshal," O'Hara said. "Thought for a moment there the vicious son of a bitch would completely lose whatever he had by way of restraint and kill me, for certain sure."

"Oh, I doubt that," Longarm offered. "He can't be stupid enough to commit bloody murder right in front of a witness."

"I don't think he saw you back there until you spoke up, Marshal. Near as I can tell, he thought the two of us were alone. As it stands right now, he didn't do any real damage. Hell, my twelve-year-old little sister can hit harder than he did today. 'Course, I wouldn't want him to catch me alone, in a dark alleyway, with a barrel stave in his hands."

From a doorway in the wall behind the table Longarm favored, a sultry female voice said, "Well, he obviously missed me as well. You know, boys, it's been my experience that such stupid oversights can easily be the cause of a man of his kind getting killed graveyard dead."

Chapter 3

Longarm and Mike O'Hara turned and watched as a high-breasted, narrow-waisted, black-haired, and ruby-lipped beauty strutted into the room. She was dressed in a tasteful blouse with a chin-tickling collar, which she wore under a dove-gray, short-waisted jacket. Her floor-length skirt swished around long legs as she marched over and laid a sawed-off shotgun on the bar.

"I heard the whole business from my window above." She motioned to an almost imperceptible glass-paned opening in the back wall over the corner of the bar. "Had it come to anything like serious gunplay, had you missed, sir, trust me, I wouldn't have." She patted the shotgun. "My big popper here wouldn't have left enough of the angry gentleman to fill an empty tobacco pouch."

O'Hara waved in the general direction of an unseen upper level and said, "Miss Cora's quarters are upstairs, Marshal Long."

The woman held out a flawlessly manicured hand, decorated with an enormous diamond-cut, topaz ring. "I'm Cora Anne Fisher, Marshal—the extremely grateful owner, operator, and unpaid protector of the Holy Moses."

Longarm snatched his hat off and, Southern gentleman that he was, bowed ever so slightly at the waist. He gently took the lady's fingers in his, stared into liquid-blue eyes, and kissed the back of her hand. He offered up his most winning smile, then said, "It is indeed my distinct pleasure, Miss Fisher."

"Oh, do call me Cora, Marshal. I must insist."

"Most certainly, but only if you'll call me Custis."

Mike O'Hara's nervous glance darted from one face to the other. Longarm noticed that the still red-faced drink slinger suddenly appeared a mite uncomfortable. Then, the bartender grabbed his towel up and said, "Well. Think I'll just wander on down to the other end of the bair. Absolutely sure you folks won't even begin to mind. See if I can't find something to wipe, while you two get better acquainted."

Longarm made a gallant motion toward the table he'd recently vacated and said, "Would you like to sit a spell, Cora?"

He watched as her eyes scanned him from toe to crown—lingering ever so briefly on his crotch. When her wide-eyed, approving gaze met his, she smiled, reached out, and grasped his arm. "You are one fine-lookin' man, Custis. Noticed as much from my perch upstairs. But, you know, while it's most kind of you to offer me a seat down here at your table, think I'd much prefer that you accompany me upstairs so I can *properly* thank you for taking care of a growing irritation—and also for keeping poor Mike from suffering any more than necessary at the hands of a brutish thug."

Longarm waved toward Cora's private door in the

back wall with his hat and said, "Lead the way, ma'am. I am your obedient servant."

As he followed the stunning woman up the narrow set of steep stairs to her living quarters, he tried but couldn't keep himself from letting his imagination run wild. The undulating roll of the eye-catching girl's wondrously shaped ass, right in his face, got Longarm to speculating on what exactly that gorgeous ass might look like when stripped naked and joyfully bouncing up and down on his rock-hard prong. Before he could even think to control the beast in his pants, it roared to snarling life and, faster than winter wind can raise dry leaves, turned into something akin to a heat-hardened steel push rod on a Baldwin steam locomotive.

A spacious combination landing and waiting area outside the door of Cora Fisher's lodgings sported a rose-colored Tiffany lamp, table, and brocaded chair. All the furnishings rested on a colorful Oriental rug resplendent with golden fire-breathing dragons.

The interior of her spacious apartment proved just as stylish, clever, and refined as her manner of dress and the decorative features of her drinking establishment below. Longarm stood in the middle of an enormous single room laid out across the entire back of the building that housed the Holy Moses Saloon. He held his hat over a throbbing, uncomfortable crotch, and marveled at the sizable space, which was divided into three completely independent, tasteful, and sophisticated living areas.

Each zone of the room was separated from the others by the simple, but elegant arrangement of its opulent furnishings. In the corner farthest from the door, the most sumptuous of the trio included the biggest bed he'd ever seen. Against the wall, behind the bed, stood a tall, colorful, Oriental screen depicting naked women in various forms of mutual sexual satisfaction. Thick Turkish carpets covered the plank floor beneath the huge bed and deadened any noise coming from below.

"Damned nice spot," he said. "You've done what appears to be a professional decorator's job on this place, Cora. Sure enough beats my pitiful lawman's digs over on Cherry Creek by a country mile."

"Why, thank you for noticing, Custis," Cora Fisher said as she made her way to a huge wardrobe, opened it and began removing her clothing. "Most men don't," she said over her now naked shoulder.

"What on earth are you doing, girl?" he asked, feeling immediately astonished and embarrassed by the awkward silliness of the question.

She threw him a brazen, lust-filled, leering glance and said, "Well, as I said before, you're about to be *properly* thanked for taking care of a gnawing problem that has plagued me for almost three weeks now, Custis. A potentially dangerous problem I had no real idea how to handle."

He dropped his Stetson on a red plush chair trimmed in gold braid and unbuckled his pistol belt. It fell to the carpet-covered floor with a dull *thump*. He strode across the room, grabbed the nearly naked girl from behind and ran his hands from her crotch up to her full, heavy breasts. She trembled, moaned, and leaned into him. He rolled her his nipples between his fingers and thumbs, as she pushed the muscular, rounded mounds of her white-hot ass against his pulsating cock.

Cora threw her head back onto Longarm's shoulder, reached down between them, grabbed the first thing she could find and breathed into his ear, "No longer than we've known each other I can already feel there's some-

22

thing wonderful growing between us, Custis. Something warm, hard, and downright *magnificent*. My God, darlin', this thing is as long as the barrel on my shotgun—and so hard a tomcat couldn't scratch it."

Longarm ran a hand back down her board-flat stomach. Muscles, all along the way, twitched and jumped under his fingers until he reached the already wet, superheated notch between her legs. When the tip of his finger hit the perfect spot, she went rigid in his arms, and squeezed his dick so hard he jerked and had to back away. "Damn, girl. I like an enthusiastic woman as much as any man, but you've got to be a bit more careful. Can't go squeezin' . . ."

She twirled around in his arms, plastered herself against him, welded her mouth to his and tried to suck the tongue right out of his head. The kiss got so intense, he thought his spurs might be coming up along with at least one other thing below his waist. Finally, she broke the lip lock with a resounding smack and whispered, "You must forgive my brazen behavior. I don't usually conduct myself like a street-walking hussy. Well, that's not exactly true. When I'm naked I just cannot seem to control my unruly passions. In truth, I've not been with a man for sometime now, and, honey, I knew as soon as I saw you downstairs that today was the day to break an almost yearlong drought."

"You know, Cora, you talk too much," he said. Then for about a minute, they ripped at each other's remaining clothing like wild, starving animals in search of food. Once they were both completely buck-assed naked, except for Cora's black velvet choker that sported a thumbnail-sized cameo, he grabbed her up in his arms and strode toward the bed.

As they passed a full-length dressing mirror, he stopped, turned toward it and held her so they could both see all the normally hidden wonders of each other that they wanted to see. He let her down to her feet, ran his hands back up to her breasts and watched her writhe under the caresses of her ample, swollen nipples. "Look at that. You are one helluva beautiful woman, Cora," he said to her image in the mirror.

"And you are one helluva beautiful man," she said, then reached down, grabbed him again, gazed at their reflections and watched as her own hand moved up and down his rigid member. She giggled, turned her head as far as she could, stuck her tongue in his ear, then whispered, "And this is one helluva beautiful cock I'm squeezing. Now, for the love of God, Custis, get on with it. Fuck me till I'm as weak as two-day-old kitten. When we finish I want to be soaking wet from the soles of my feet to the top of my head."

He jerked her around so they faced each other and grabbed a cheek of her ass in each hand. "Not only do you talk too much, but you've got one really nasty mouth on you, girl."

She pulled his head down and stuck her tongue in his ear again, then whispered, "You don't know the half of it—yet—big boy."

He'd held off as long as he could. Longarm snatched Cora up in his arms, hustled across the room and pitched her onto the enormous bed. She landed on her back, legs spread as far apart as humanly possible, knees all the way up against her ears. He crawled on top of her and plunged his heat-hardened rod into the steaming, wet depths so shamelessly offered up for his unfettered, carnal pleasure.

Cora threw one arm around his neck, got her mouth

24

next to his ear once more and whispered, "Talk nasty, darlin'. Come on, baby, I want to hear the words, not just feel them."

For nearly two hours, Longarm tried every trick he'd ever learned from every woman he'd ever known. They moved from the bed to the carpeted floor. From the floor to the red chair. From the chair to a spot against the wall—where pictures clattered, broke loose, and fell to the floor. From the wall to the top of her vanity. Never once, for even an instant, did they come uncoupled.

He fully exhausted his extensive vocabulary of smutty, coarse, vulgar, and lewd language at least three times. When he finally hit on what appeared to be a favorite fantasy of Cora's, one that involved the possibility of having another woman join in on the festivities, the girl seemed to come unhinged. The bucking, snorting, yelping conclusion to their dance of unbridled, furniture-rattling pleasure took place inside the wardrobe on top of all the clothing they'd knocked loose from the hangers.

During one final, gushing, orgasmic convulsion she squealed, "Oh! Oh! Oh! Ummmmm! Sweet Jesus!" and collapsed into a pulsating, sweaty, sex-drenched heap.

Longarm lifted the girl out of the wardrobe, fell back into the bed with her and drifted off into exhausted slumber. He awoke sometime later and felt as though the anonymous "insurance salesman" had whipped his ass with a knotted rope.

With great devotion to the effort, Cora was ardently trying to suck him back into a state of readiness for more in the way of wildly sensual pleasures. He ran his fingers into her hair and pulled her away. "You've gotta give it a rest, darlin'. I really can't stay much longer."

She strained to get free of his grip and managed to run

her tongue around the head of his dick till he was compelled to force her away from her efforts for a second time. "Well," she said, her head resting on his chest, "are you hungry, by any chance?"

"Damn right. My insides feel like a rain barrel during an Arizona drought."

The seemingly energized girl hopped from the bed like a startled deer, padded barefoot and naked across the room, cracked open the little window over the bar, then called out, "Mike, would you bring up a tray of food, please. You can leave it on the table outside my door."

During the entirety of a badly needed break for refreshments, rest, and recuperation, Longarm was forced to fight off Cora's continuing advances. When he had to pull her from under the table, he decided it was about time to take his leave.

"Much as I hate to," he said later, pulling her hands from inside his pants, as he tried to button up, "I've got to be headin' out. Have to swing by my room, get all my gear ready, try to get at least some sleep, then head out real early tomorrow morning on the train for Tascosa."

Clearly disappointed by the unexpected news, Cora watched him strap his pistol belt back on, then whined, "Tascosa? What on earth's in Tascosa? I'm here, darlin' and, as you can well see, more'n ready." Still stark naked, she snuggled up against him again, grabbed his crotch, and tried her best to massage him into compliance once more. "Stay here for the night. You can get all your ole stuff tomorrow morning and still make the train. Can't you?"

He grasped her by the shoulders and held her at arm's length. "Tell you what. Soon as I get back from this trip, I'll be right at your door knocking. I promise."

She ran her tongue across her lips and began playing with herself. "If you stick around, I'll find another woman to spend the night with us," she said and rubbed herself against him. "Already have someone in mind. In fact, I've had her in mind for quite a while now. Problem in the past was I've never believed most men could deal with the prospect of bedding two women at the same time. Being as how you've proven you're not most men, I think it could be a lot of fun."

"God Almighty, girl. That's a hard one to pass on. Tell you what. You make all the arrangements, and we'll do exactly that when I get back."

"Promise," she said, then sucked her finger and did a little-girl act.

He pulled her finger out of her mouth, "I promise," he said, kissed her, then started for the door.

"Not that one," she said and pointed to a richly curtained wall opposite the foot of the bed. "There's a door behind the drape that leads directly down a closed staircase to the outside. Best you use it—from now on."

Once on the street and headed for his own room, he stopped long enough to light a cheroot. He flipped the match into the gutter, shook his head in wonder at the previous few hours of wildly sensual distraction. Under his breath he said, "Jesus, just never know what you're gonna get when it comes to women."

Chapter 4

Two days after Cora Anne Fisher strapped herself around Longarm's waist—and almost rode him into the Turkish carpets covering her bedroom floor—the haggard, coach-weary, deputy marshal stepped off the Denver, Texas, and Fort Worth Railroad's passenger train onto a barely perceptible loading platform. The structure appeared so new the lumber still oozed sap, even though a bracing cold permeated the damp air.

Chilling, ice-tinged winds from the west kept a sandy cloud of topsoil whipping around his ears and deposited a powder-fine layer of grime all over everything within sight. Longarm flipped up the collar of his suit coat, buttoned it to the neck, and pulled on a pair of leather ropers. Nearby, a skinny baggage clerk named Ike Pepper, with whom he'd shared a cigar on the trip down from Trinidad, unloaded his possibles bag, bedroll, McClellan saddle, and other necessary equipment.

Longarm cast a squinty-eyed glance at the outhouse-sized Tascosa ticket agent's shack and shook his head. "That's the closest thing to nothin' for a depot building

29

I've ever seen. Can't even imagine how the agent gets a stove in there."

Ike Pepper threw Longarm's saddle onto the platform, placed clenched fists on bony hips, then said, "Sure ain't much, is she. You know, way I've got it figured, Marshal, the Denver, Texas, and Fort Worth probably won't even have a real physical stopping place in these parts a few years down the road."

As he studied the area with a bit more in the way of concentrated interest, Longarm realized the railroad's minuscule station building—such as it was—a livery, and a few crude adobe shacks were the only structures in sight. He waved at the empty horizon. "Where the hell's the town, Ike? Shit, I've been through Tascosa a time or two, and, near as I can remember, this ain't it."

The clerk grinned, let out a burst of cackling laughter, then pointed north. "Oh she's still here. 'Bout two miles over yonder way, as the crow flies. 'Tother side of the Canadian River. You can see 'er if'n you strain a bit. Usually puts off a kinda cloudy piece of haze over them trees along Tascosa Creek. Just follow the cattle trail headin' north to Dodge. Cain't miss it."

Longarm danced in a complete circle, arms out, palms turned toward heaven, as though unbelieving. "You mean the damned railroad totally missed the existing town?"

"Yessir. That she did. Damned hard to figure, ain't it. Just never have been able to reckon out exactly how them folks back east in the main office arrive at such monumentally stupid determinations. Some of the natives, here 'bouts, have gone and named this mess a-growin' up around our purported depot New Tascosa. But, you know, Marshal, I'd be willin' to bet everthang I've got in my pockets that neither one of these places is even gonna exist twenty year from now."

Longarm scratched his head in shocked amazement, then pulled two square-cut cheroots from his coat pocket and handed one to the railroader. He fired a match and lit both smokes. The men puffed their stogies to life and stared at the seemingly endless, empty, windblown plains stretching all the way from Amarillo to Kansas and beyond. "Well, Ike, I have to admit, I ain't no businessman. But building around a fine little town like Tascosa—as though it never even existed—now, that is a damned strange business decision, if I've ever heard tell of one. Sometimes you see stuff like this and realize it's often harder'n hell to figure out what the idiot fuckers educated at Harvard's business school, who make it to the top of major corporations, are thinkin'."

The engineer leaned out an open window, glanced toward the caboose, then announced departure for all points south by blowing his whistle several times and venting off rolling clouds of steam. A few seconds later, the huge DT&FW's smoke-belching Baldwin engine chuffed to fire-breathing life. Giant spinning wheels grabbed at the cold steel rails, and the train crawled forward like an iron turtle gaining speed.

Ike Pepper grinned and waved from the baggage coach doorway, as each of the train cars slowly snapped into place, and jerked along behind the straining engine. "Maybe I'll see you on the trip back this way, Marshal Long," he shouted.

"Yeah. Probably will. But I'm not real sure when that'll be, Ike. Given what I can see from here, right now, hope it's a helluva lot sooner than later."

Except for the old McClellan saddle, Longarm left all

his traps in the protective care of the local ticket agent, until he could rent a ride and return. He walked to the livery and, after several minutes of careful examination, picked out a long-legged iron-gray mare named Buttercup.

"Might not even need a horse while I'm here, but I want one handy just in case I do," Longarm said to the stable owner.

"Well, friend, don't let this here animal's name fool you," the stoop-shouldered, hawk-nosed hostler said, as he led the gray from its stall. "She damned sure ain't no plow horse. Ole Buttercup has been known to get right rambunctious on occasion."

"That a fact?"

"Yessir. She's thrown more'n a few greenhorns what let down their guard. Even ran me into a barbed-wire fence once. Swear she done it on purpose. Damn near sliced my boot off. Hateful bitch has a well-earned reputation as a biter, too. She'll happily take a plug outta you the size of an apple 'fore you can bat an eye."

"Maybe you should've named her something else."

"Like what?"

"Don't know. But since you mentioned it, maybe, Hateful Bitch would've been a better handle. Has a nice ring to it. Kinda gets the message across, too, don't it?"

The hostler scratched his stubble-covered chin for a second, then said, "Yeah. Sure does. But you know, bet I'd never be able to rent the fractious devil again if I named her somethin' like Hateful Bitch. Besides, my daughter named the hoss, and she'd have a cat if'n I changed it to Hateful Bitch. Not sure my wife'd like it much either. She's a church-goin' woman, you know. She hates that word *bitch*. Don't hold with takin' the strain off'n yore liver, swearin', and such like. Try to do all my dadblastin' and consarnin' when she ain't around close 'nuff to hear any of it."

"Well, then, why'd you bother to tell me about Buttercup?"

"Just bein' neighborly, friendly-like as it were. Now if'n you wuz a greenhorn, I prolly wouldna said a word."

"I see. Well, don't really matter none, to tell the truth. I've always preferred a nag with some spirit," Longarm said, then grinned and pitched the aptly nicknamed Old Ball Buster saddle onto the animal's back.

Buttercup's stringy-muscled owner made a retching sound like a cat trying to hack up a hairball the size of a horse collar. He shook his head and said, "What in the blue-eyed hell are you doin', mister?"

"As you can plainly see. I'm saddlin' the lovely and peaceable Miss Buttercup for our short ride to heavenly Tascosa. What else?"

The stableman swept his hat off and slapped his leg with it before stuffing the floppy thing back on his hairless head. "Sweet Jesus, save me from the unintended influence of mo-rons," he said. "See here now, my friend, that damned thing you just put on her back was designed by a sadistic fool. The ignert son of a bitch couldn't lead an army for shit and, evidently, had some sort of hidden hatred in his wizened heart for every man what served under his command, and every single one of them as followed."

"Well, now, all that might be true, but you have to admit, this saddle's mighty easy on the horse."

"That's a highly debatable piece of faulty fuckin' reasonin', if'n I ever heard one. Hell's bells, boy, I served under the man who invented that damned thing at both of them Bull Run dust-ups. Look, a two-hundred-year-old war saddle favored by them Spanish lancers, as went through

33

this country lookin' for El Dorado, was comfortable for the horse, too. That still don't make it a great idea for the rider."

"Well, you're right as rain about the rider business. Don't call 'em 'ball busters' for nothing."

"Here. This 'uns a well-broke California," the hostler said, as he turned to the nearest stall rail, then pulled a handsome tooled leather seat down and handed it to Longarm. "She's light, only ten pounds. Easy as a satin pillow on man and beast. Trust me on this. You'll think you're at home in your favorite rockin' chair. And hell, you can have it for no extra charge during your entire stay. Feller what owned it ain't got no more use fer it, anyways."

"Oh, and why's that?"

"Well, he went and got his poor dumb ass throwed into the Canadian from a eighty-foot bluff, down river a few miles. Happened 'bout a month ago. Poor sumbitch musta tried to break the fall with his head. He landed on a rock the size of a buckboard, then bounced a couple a times 'fore he landed in the river and proceeded to drown."

Longarm glanced back and forth between the saddles for several seconds. "All right, I'll go along with you this time, but only if I can leave the McClellan here till my business here is finished."

"Oh, hell, yes. Take the California, son. God Almighty, but I just cain't stand to see a feller make hisself downright miserably uncomfortable for no good fuckin' reason."

"Thought you said you didn't do no cussin' round here 'cause of your wife."

"Oh. Well, she ain't here right now. That'n, and the other'n a while back, just kinda slipped out by accident, goddammit. Man has to vent his liver ever once in a while, don't you think?"

Atop a windblown, grass-covered bluff overlooking the Canadian River, Longarm sat the gray and scrutinized the shallow stream's thousand-year-old crossing point. On the far side, the rooftops and chimneys of Tascosa were now clearly visible. Nearly surrounded by a ring of sheltering hills, the rough village, comprised mostly of small adobe buildings and similar coarse homes, sat astride a sluggish creek lined with enormous cottonwoods and stately elms. Most of the leaves had gone yellow, soon to turn a brilliant gold, as the winds sweeping down from the northern plains sharpened with winter's jagged edge.

Longarm patted the mare on the neck, and said, "Now this is more like it, Buttercup. I remember this spot from my previous trips. Should be an easy wade across to the other side from here."

He urged the mare into the sluggish, slow-moving river. She sloshed through ugly, rust-colored, knee-deep water, then easily scrambled up the sandy bank on the far side. First thing he noticed, once they'd crested the bank, was a desolate-looking cemetery. Godforsaken spot was populated by a sad collection of scattered wooden grave markers, sitting on a rock-littered hilltop that overlooked a sharp, curving bend in the Canadian.

"Looks like someone's been adding to the population of Boot Hill, since my last visit," Longarm mumbled to himself, then pulled out a cheroot and lit it. He breathed a lung of smoke into the heavy, cold air and mumbled, "More markers than I remember." He shook his head at the sad prospect of spending eternity in such a bleak and mournful place, then urged the gray on toward town.

Man and beast moseyed through a drooping stand of cottonwoods and headed down an easy slope toward the largest concentration of buildings, located a good quarter of a mile off. Here and there along the way, a lone, ruddy-faced child played in the grassless yard of his parent's rude dwelling. On several occasions, the pale, sad face of a suspicious woman appeared at a window or door, only to vanish back into the darkness of her raw home's inky interior. Skinny dogs darted from favored hiding places, bared their yellow teeth, barked, snapped, then ran from the strange man and his ghostly gray mount.

Longarm waded Buttercup over the nearly dry bed of Tascosa Creek and, almost immediately, hit the west end of the main thoroughfare leading into the town's bustling business district. Wagons, horses, and local citizens flowed back and forth in a steady stream along the dusty street. Some tipped their hats. Some waved. Others milled about in small groups under the shelter provided by a convenient tree, talking, laughing, and smoking. Seemed a mite on the busy side for a weekday, he thought.

As Longarm and the horse made their way down the broad, sandy path, they passed almost fifty residences, a livery stable, a bake shop, a saddle maker's operation, and at least two cow-country watering holes. He knew if they stayed on Main and kept going east, the rugged shacks of Tascosa's red-light district, called Hogtown by the natives, would have quickly come into view about a quarter of a mile outside town.

He reined up in front of a coarse-looking adobe building squatting amid a grove of cottonwoods. He recognized the rough structure as the single largest edifice in town. A sign, enhanced with the sun-bleached skull of an enormous longhorn steer, hung directly over the front door, and boldly proclaimed the rugged accommodations as the Exchange Hotel. Longarm dismounted and stepped across the crude threshold.

A desk clerk, Longarm had never seen on any of his prior stopovers, flashed a snaggletoothed smile, as the tired lawman strode up to the ramshackle desk.

The inn's toothy greeter, who sported a gray-tinted mustache and beard that made him look like he'd swallowed a two-foot section of a ratty, aged buffalo rug, twirled his leather-bound register around for easy customer access. "Welcome to the Exchange Hotel. You are entering Tascosa's finest lodgings, sir. Texas cattle buyer, I'd bet," the man said and held out an already dipped pen. "I can spot you fellers easy as eatin' my ma's fresh-baked apple pie. Some say I've something akin to second sight. And, sir, you have the look of a successful cattleman. Prosperous-like, I'd say."

A surprising number of bored-looking, brush poppers loafed around the modest lobby's well-stoked, potbellied stove. Most smoked slim Mexican cigars and worked at adding to a communal pile of wood shavings on the floor at their feet. Dressed in the garb of common cowboys, several of the whittlers glanced up to casually note the stranger's arrival, but then went back to their whittle-and-spit efforts as though totally lacking in anything that approached common curiosity. Some paid no attention to Longarm at all, and one or two of the supremely uninterested slept with wide-brimmed hats pulled over snoring faces.

The presumptuous clerk watched with more than a bit of interest as Longarm scratched his name, city of origin, and business in the dog-eared ledger. "Ah, well bless my soul. A deputy U.S. marshal, no less. Guess my powers of observation are getting a mite rusty. From Denver, by Godfrey. Guess you're here for the trial," he said, and appeared to grimace.

Longarm glanced around the room and realized by the next morning everyone in Tascosa would very likely know he'd arrived, and have more than a good idea what his business would entail. While it really didn't matter one way or the other, he usually felt better if he could maintain something akin to a low profile. He stifled a growing feeling of irritation with the mouthy clerk handling the hotel's register and forced a tense smile.

"Actually, Marshal, you'll have to forgive a bit of prevarication on my part. We at the Exchange have been expecting you. Didn't know your name, but we'd been made aware of your possible arrival."

Somewhat surprised by the revelation, Longarm grunted, "Really?"

"Yes. You see," the gregarious clerk reached under the counter between them, produced an envelope, and handed it to Longarm, "I've a note for you, sir. Delivered by visiting Judge Henry Cain, as I recall." An undercurrent of strain accompanied Cain's name. "The judge left it with strict instructions that I was to see you got it as quickly as possible upon your arrival. His honor appeared right concerned 'bout me making sure you had it, in hand, at your earliest convenience."

Longarm held the mysterious missive between a finger and thumb and stared at it for several seconds. No name appeared on the envelope, only the inscription *Arriving Deputy Marshal*. He slid the still sealed note into his jacket pocket and said, "Well, now, guess you can put

Judge Cain's mind at ease, next time you see him. Think I'll read it later."

"As you deem appropriate, Marshal. The judge did also request that we inform him of your arrival, as well."

"Do tell. Figured I'd talk with the man tomorrow morning anyway. Might be just as well that he knows I'm here as quickly as possible, I suppose. Now, the room, if you please, sir."

The convivial clerk pulled a key from a pegboard on the wall and slid it across the battered countertop. "Goin' rate these days is fifty cents a night for the room. Same amount for meals. That's if you should choose to eat with us, Marshal. Your accommodations are located at the end of 'at 'ere hall yonder—next to the last room on the left. Judge Cain has the one right next door. Wanted you close at hand it appears."

"I see. Well, that's fine with me," Longarm mumbled and took the proffered key to room number five. "Long as the space has a bed in it's all I really care about. First thing I need though is a livery stall where I can put my mount during the course of my stay."

"Oh, I can take care of that for you if you'd like, Marshal Long. We have a boy on call at all times to do just that very thing. After seeing that your possibles, bedroll, rifle, and such, get delivered to your room, he'll walk the animal down to Micky McCormick's place on the corner. I'm absolutely certain Micky's people will make sure the beast gets the best of care. We can even add the stable fee to your final billing here at the hotel, if that meets with your approval."

"Sounds just fine as frog hair, but make sure you let the boy know that the gray tied just outside your door has been known to bite. And have him inform the hostler that I'd like the animal kept at the ready during my stay here, just in case I need it quick. Perhaps more important, for the moment at any rate, I would be most obliged if you could direct me to a good saloon. Spotted several likely looking prospects, as I rode into town, but will defer to your judgment in the matter, Mr. ahhhhh, sorry, but I didn't get *your* name."

The clerk flashed a grateful smile, then served up a deferential, albeit strained, nod, held out his hand, and said, "Chauncy Pedigrew, Marshal Long." Once they'd shook and nodded, Pedigrew pointed to the entryway and said, "Just go back outside and turn to your immediate right. Waterin' hole named the Cattle Exchange is only a few steps from our front door, as a matter of pure fact. 'Course there's the Jenkins and Dunn across Main, as well. But, I'd bet you'll like the Equity Bar better."

"The Equity Bar, huh? Must admit, it has been a few years since my last visit to Tascosa. Don't remember that one."

"Yessir. Well, it's just the kind of place I think a man of your experience and taste would really appreciate. A bit on the rustic side, if you catch my meaning. Three doors down on this side of the street, 'tother side of King's Drug Store. Bartender's a healthy-lookin', ruddy-faced, friendly gent named Jackson Hooper. Fine feller. Never been known to short-shot a customer."

Longarm put a finger to the brim of his Stetson. "If Judge Cain shows up, I'd be most grateful if you'd just direct him to the Equity. Would imagine I'll be there for a spell." He nodded, then turned and stepped back out onto Tascosa's Main Street.

A copper-colored sun hung a hand's breadth above an

inflamed horizon. While lighting a cheroot behind a cupped hand, Longarm took special note of the North Star Restaurant located next door to Cone and Duran's Mercantile, directly across the thoroughfare from the hotel entrance. Might have to try the North Star for breakfast some morning, he thought, then heeled it for the Equity Bar. His extended dry spell on the train from Denver required immediate and devoted attention.

Chapter 5

More a cantina than an actual saloon, compared to Cora Fisher's Holy Moses back in Denver, Tascosa's bustling Equity Bar was as rough as a shucked cob. A pack of ten or fifteen indolent hounds littered the bare ground around the front door. One jowly red bone raised its massive head, snorted, flopped a ragged tail in the dust, then dropped right back off to sleep. Most of the lazy bunch barely moved enough to take notice as Longarm picked his way through their lethargic midst. He stepped over the threshold of an already open front entrance, which was obviously in sore need of a screened door, and into the barebones operation.

A four-foot-tall, twenty-foot-long, marble-topped liquor counter ran along the entirety of the westernmost wall. The crowded bar flaunted the deep scars of severe abuse, most of which could be directly attributed to the careless treatment of its rough, brush-popping, Mexican-spur-wearing cowboy clientele.

Much to Longarm's initial dismay, the Equity's back bar appeared sparsely stocked. But when he finally leaned through a shoulder-to-shoulder wall of milling leather pounders, waved the round-faced drink slinger over, and ordered a double shot of Maryland rye, he found himself pleasantly surprised by the quality of the tonsil paint the eternally smiling bartender poured.

"Mighty fine, Mr. Hooper," Longarm said as he hoisted his glass in salute.

The beaming liquor dispenser nodded vigorously. "Always try our best to please a thirsty customer, sir. Hope you enjoy it. Take a seat anywhere you choose to light. I'll keep an eye out and bring a refill anytime you like. All you have to do is raise your empty glass, and I'll be there on the double."

Longarm carried the brimming drink to an empty table in the farthest corner of the room near the back exit. He pushed a well-used chair up against the wall so it faced the front door, then flopped into it.

In a matter of minutes, the relaxing, congenial atmosphere, laced with the pungent bouquet from a thick cloud of cigar and cigarette smoke, ample giggle juice, and a rarely swept floor littered with a layer of freshly rendered sawdust, worked its special magic. The bone-weary fatigue he felt, from his two-day train trip seated on a thinly padded bench fashioned by demons in what he pictured as a hellish workshop, drained to the farthest reaches of his body, elbowed aside by fine rye whiskey.

By the time Longarm's third double hit the table, he'd loosened up considerably and felt pretty damned good. The fresh drink had barely christened his eager lips when a tall, tastefully turned-out gent in a two-hundred-dollar suit, brilliantly white shirt, scarlet cravat, and diamond stick pin, strolled up to the table, placed a hand on the doweled back of an empty chair, and sat down before he bothered to say, "Mind if I take a seat, Marshal?"

Longarm waved consent with his glass. "Been waitin' for you, Judge. Figured you'd be right along when that nosy feller down at the Exchange Hotel mentioned somethin' 'bout informin' you of my arrival."

Judge Henry Cain removed his stylish and spotlessly clean beaver hat, dropped it on the table, and took the seat nearest Longarm's corner nest. With practiced ceremony, he shook loose a leonine head of hair, then ran his fingers through the shoulder-length silver tresses like a fussy woman consumed in her own vanity. He seemed determined not to make eye contact and further disappointed Longarm by failing to offer his hand to shake.

A pompous, finger-snapping motion from Cain, directed at the bustling, sweat-covered bartender, got an instant response. While the dandified adjudicator never uttered a single audible word, a glass of absinthe got smartly delivered to the table.

Longarm's eyes widened. "By God, I'm surprised you can even get that stuff way the hell out here in the Texas panhandle country, Judge," he said.

Cain barely wet his lips with the sickly sweet liquor, but appeared to savor the taste. "To the contrary, Marshal. When it comes to the vast variety of *espiritus fermenti* a man can employ to thoroughly decimate his mind and body, I've discovered that, even as remote as this rough way station might appear, Tascosa is most cosmopolitan." He took another barely perceptible sip from the glass, then licked his lips. "Chauncy Pedigrew was, of course, the very person who informed me of your recent arrival, Marshal Long."

Longarm raised his glass again. "Appeared a man of his word. Said he would. Gave me no reason not to believe him."

Cain daintily flicked an errant crumb of some sort off the table top, as though disposing of something akin to porcine fecal matter. He jerked a handkerchief that matched his shirt in radiance from his coat pocket, dusted a spot on the table, then leaned on a stylish elbow. "Have no complaint about the liquor, but, my God, the place is a disgusting dump when compared to the lowliest of dram shops back in Amarillo. Did you read my note, Marshal Long?" he said with a sniff.

"Must admit I haven't got around to 'er yet, Judge," Longarm said, then flashed a sheepish grin by way of wordless apology.

"And why not, if I might be so bold as to inquire?"

"Well, as a matter of pure fact, I only got it placed in my hands little more than an hour and a half ago. Besides, right now I'm busier'n hell drinkin'. Outside of your envelope displayed no indication of urgency, so, I figured whatever the communication contained could wait until tomorrow mornin'."

Cain made a noise that sounded to Longarm kind of like harrumph, harrumph, harrumph, then almost gagged when he snorted, "That's exactly the kind of attitudinal laxness I feared might manifest itself in the person sent to protect my life."

Longarm casually pulled a cheroot from his vest pocket, fired the tobacco with a sulfur match, then said, "Well, now, that's a shade on the harsh side, don't you think, Judge?"

"Not under the present set of circumstances."

"And what set of circumstances are those?"

"Well, sweet Jesus, I'm sure Marshal Vail informed you that my life has been threatened."

"Absolutely. That he did. That he did, indeed. But you

appear very much alive and undamaged, Judge. Been sittin' here tryin', but I can't seem to spot any bullet holes, bruises, or even a scratch on your person—unless, perhaps, my recent stagger juice consumption has seriously clouded a normally keen sense of the obvious. Can't remember a time in the past when I mistook a dead man for a live one. But there's a first time for everything, I suppose."

Cain's patrician face screwed itself into a mask of condemnation. "I do not think your current assignment is, in the least, grounds for levity, Marshal Long. My presence in this world appears to be in imminent danger. Over the past few weeks, as a result of repeated threats, I have grown to fear the worst possible outcome for my participation in the Tull affair."

Longarm gifted himself with an inward smile, then returned Judge Cain's pompous remarks in kind. "Am I to take it that you've received more communiqués expressing pointed displeasure at your continued existence?"

"Yes." With considerable self-serving ceremony, Cain pulled a neatly stacked pile of paper tied with twine from an inside coat pocket and pitched it on the table.

Longarm riffled through the stack and briefly glanced at each of seven separate notes. He found most of the short, crude messages were the same and merely repeated a nebulous threat of dire consequences should Cain prove bold enough to turn up in Tascosa. "Not very original are they? But, it does appear somebody has bloody plans in mind for you, Judge—a fact that we could probably apply to nearly every black-robed adjudicator in the west, at the moment. But, you know, there's something right odd here."

Cain's eyes darted back and forth from the thin pile of

papers to Longarm's face for several seconds before he snapped, "What? What's *odd*? I didn't notice anything *odd*. Threats of brutal murder might be construed as a good many things, I am not certain *odd* would qualify as one of them. I'm especially mortified by the one note that graphically describes what the writer has in mind for my balls. Sweet Merciful Father, can't even imagine such a horrific thing."

Longarm dropped an authoritative finger on the stack of threats. "Yeah, well, I guess havin' some anonymous person threaten to stuff your very own personal *huevos* in your mouth and set 'em on fire would get just about anybody's attention. But, what I'm sayin' is, there's no mention of the trial, or Bronson Tull, or Rufus Tull, or any of the Tulls for that matter, Judge. Not a single word about 'em in this stuff."

Cain shook his head as though he'd been slapped. "My God, Marshal. You're absolutely right, and I didn't even notice the discrepancy." He snatched up his hat and fanned himself with it. "Here I've been worried to the point of distraction over this trial and there might well be no connection between the two things whatsoever. I'm astounded by my lack of recognition."

A buzz of edgy commotion and nervous movement near the Equity's front entrance turned both men's attention away from Cain's collection of menacing notes, and their nascent discussion of them. A tall, sunburnt, white-bearded gent wearing chaps, a leather vest, a thigh-length canvas jacket, and a Boss of the Plains hat with a flat-tened brim in the style of those worn by Moseby's Civil War rangers, filled the doorway like an angry storm cloud boiling across the North Texas plains with thunder and lightning.

Fragments of the dying day filtered in from outside, squeezed around the man's hulking form and dropped to the floor in splotches of fading red and gold. A thick braided-leather quirt dangled from his wrist. He slapped the abbreviated whip against a cavalry-booted leg several times. In a matter of seconds, the busy cantina got quieter than the bottom of a fresh dug grave at midnight.

"Oh, my word." Cain wheezed.

"I'll just be damned," Longarm added under his breath, then stealthily slid his Colt Frontier model pistol into his lap beneath the table. "Unless I miss my guess, Judge, that's none other than Rufus Tull."

Cain's drink-filled hand trembled for just a second, and the corner of his mouth twitched. "Oh, that's him all right, Marshal Long. Ole Rufus and I have had less than cordial dealings in the past, down in Amarillo. The man is nefarious, as well as dangerous, and often unpredictable. Old son of a bitch is damn well capable of just about anything, up to and including waving a Bible in your face like a Baptist tent revivalist to get sympathy for his reprehensible ways. Rufus Tull and the truth have never danced. Fact is I don't think ole Rufus would know the truth if it walked up and slapped him nekkid. The son we're about to put on trial is a good deal like his obstinate, belligerent, dishonest father. That familial resemblance in personality is exactly why young Bronson's in jail for murder, as we speak."

The elder Tull's piercing stare swept the smoke-filled cantina and landed on Judge Henry Cain like an anvil dropped from Heaven's front doorstep. Cowboys, some well-lubricated tipplers, and townsmen of every sort tucked tail and scurried to the nearest perceived area of safety, as Tull strode majestically to the back of the room.

Solid-silver Mexican rowels, the size of ten-dollar gold pieces, jingled and sang a pleasing song as he stomped to within a few feet of Longarm's table. Tiny, twisting cyclones of dust swirled around his fancy-booted feet amid the shavings on the unfinished plank floor.

Tull came to a swaying stop within arm's reach of Henry Cain. With a snarl of disdain, he stared down at the dapper judge and slapped the quirt across a gloved palm. "Evenin', Henry."

"Rufus."

"Guess you know why I'm here."

"Of course, I know why you're here. Bronson's trial starts day after tomorrow. I had no doubt you'd make an appearance at some point. Besides, you always were one for the grand entrance."

Tull ignored the mildly cutting remark and his knifelike gaze swung to Longarm. "Who's your friend, Henry?"

Before Cain could reply, Longarm returned Tull's glare in kind and said, "Well, whoever I might be, I'm not mute. My sainted mother taught me how to speak for myself, in real, honest-to-God, plain fuckin' English. So, why don't you ask me?"

At the corner of one of Tull's icy-gray eyes, Longarm spotted an almost imperceptible twitch. Ever so slightly, a thin, caustic grin barely split the man's lips. "You're a feisty son of a bitch, ain't you?"

Longarm's pupils drew up smaller than pieces of bird shot. "You don't know me well enough to call me a son of a bitch, mister."

The burly rancher forced a broader and even more bitter smile. "Don't know you at all, shit-kicker, but I'll call you whatever the fuck I please."

Henry Cain raised one hand in a peacemaker's gesture. "Now, now, now, gents. Let's not let the dance get out of hand so early in the festivities. There's plenty of time for you two to tangle. You should take care though, Rufus. This man is a deputy U.S. marshal from Denver." Beneath the table, Longarm cocked his pistol.

Tull let out a disgusted snort. "You think I give a burlap bag of rotten cow shit who this mouthy piece of trash is?"

Of a sudden, Judge Cain's delivery changed and became more officious. "Well, you'd damn well better care, Rufus. He's here to make sure nothing wayward happens to me during the course of your son's upcoming trial. Marshal Long has my complete faith, along with the U.S. marshal's official directions, and my personal permission to kill anyone who threatens my health or well-being."

"Well, I'll just be royally damned. A bodyguard, Henry? You went and got your own personal, federal gunman and professional killer for a bodyguard?"

"You're not listening to me, Rufus. I've already told you, threats have been made against my life. Marshal Long's mission is simply to see to my safety."

Tull swelled up like a bayou-dwelling, East Texas bullfrog. "Ain't no skin off'n my nose, lest maybe you're a thinkin' them threats came from me."

"I have no idea where they came from. Don't particularly care one way or the other. The mere fact that someone thinks he can threaten a judge of my prominence is what bothers me."

"Well, I'm damned glad to hear you ain't blamin' me for 'em threats. 'Cause you know, just as sure as the cow ate the cabbage, when I have a problem, with anyone or anything, I git right up on my hind legs and confront it directly—eyeball to eyeball, so to speak. None of that sneakin' around in the dark. Don't have no need to be sending anonymous notes, or nothing."

"Well, that's good to hear, because such behavior wouldn't help Bronson's cause in the least."

"And that leads me to why I'm here right now, Judge. Went to check on my boy, and that deputy you've got guardin' him over in Oldham County's spankin' new jail won't let me in. Says you've gotta approve any visits. That the way of it?"

"Yes, that is the way of it. But to show you my heart's in the right place, Marshal Long and I will be most happy to walk you over and see that you get to visit the boy."

Tull appeared to relax a bit. "Well, that's mighty neighborly of you, Henry. When can we do it?"

"Right now, if you'd like. I think our meeting is finished, and I've got nothing else planned for the evening. We can stroll over to the jail, and I'll see to it that you have your visit with Bronson."

Cain hopped up, stuffed his hat back on, and officiously motioned for his newly acquired bodyguard to follow suit.

Longarm hunched forward, let the hammer down on the pistol, and slid the weapon back into its holster before he pushed the chair away from the table and stood. Thank God, he thought. Sure would have hated to ruin a pleasant evening with a bloody gunfight.

Chapter 6

The unlikely trio, lawman, judge, and angry father, stepped into the deepening twilight of Tascosa's main east-west thoroughfare. Hunched in the wind, they heeled their way toward McMasters Street. A fingernail-sized slice of bloodred sun slashed across the horizon beneath a slate-colored sky smeared with a greasy patina of high, thin, black-tinted clouds.

The bone-chilling wind had freshened and blew steadily out of the west. The creeping cold had grown teeth and gained the power to weasel its way through all but the heaviest of outer garments. Longarm flipped his collar up again and stuffed his hands into the suit jacket's pockets. He wished he'd had the forethought to wear his heavy coat.

Tull slapped a booted leg with his quirt, over and over again, as he bulled his way down the middle of the rutted roadway. "Gettin' damned chilly out here, boys" he said. "Bet we'll have a hard freeze on 'fore mornin'."

At the corner of Main and McMasters, the men turned north and headed for Court Street. A block ahead, the recently constructed stone, two-story Oldham County

Courthouse and menacing iron-barred jail loomed in the twilight on opposite corners from each other. Scrawny trees of varying heights surrounded both buildings.

Cain led the party into the still spanking-new sheriff's office. A well-stoked fire blazed in an iron potbellied stove in one corner. The warmth proved most welcoming after more than ten minutes of legging it in the unexpected chill.

A napping deputy, seated behind the sheriff's desk with his feet propped up, snapped to wobbly attention. Rufus Tull stomped over to the stove and started warming his hands. The deputy blinked sleep away from baggy eyes, ran a hand over his freckled face in an effort to arouse himself, then placed a nervous hand on the Colt pistol strapped high on his narrow waist.

Henry Cain dismissed the anxious deputy's defensive action with a curt wave of the hand, then said, "No need for alarm, Nate." He made an imperious motion toward his companions and said, "This *gentleman* is Rufus Tull. Tall chap by the door is Deputy U.S. Marshal Custis Long from Denver. Rufus, Custis, this young gentleman is Sheriff Jim Best's deputy, Nate Brice. Mr. Tull's here to call on his son, Nate. You have my permission to allow him inside the cell block for a single fifteen-minute visit."

Tull turned on Cain like a caged badger with a hot poker up its butt. "You never said nothin' 'bout no measly-assed fifteen minutes, goddammit. Hell, that ain't long enough for nothin'. Ain't seen my boy since you sons of bitches snatched him outta the calaboose in Amarillo and dragged him all the way up here to this god-forsaken, windblown hunk of nuthin' three weeks ago."

Cain stood his ground and didn't blink. "You've got fifteen minutes, Rufus, or you can just forget about seeing him at all. That's my final word on the matter. Now, what's it going to be? Do you want the time? If not, don't let the door hit you in the ass on your way out."

Tull swayed back and forth like an angry grizzly on the verge of uprooting a tree, pawed at the floor with his foot, then smacked the desk with the quirt. The impact from the lick sounded like a pistol shot. "You're an irritatin' son of a bitch, Henry. You know that, don't you?"

"So you've told me on more than one occasion in the past. Now, strip that coat off and let Marshal Long search you, or get the hell out of Sheriff Best's jail."

Tull's face went scarlet. "Search me? I'll just be goddamned if your personal attack dog's gonna search me."

A wicked grin sliced across Cain's face. His lips curled back in a deliberate sneer. "Well, Rufus, you've been living in a make-believe world if you think for a single second that I'd let you in the cell block without being searched. My God, man, you could carry a Napoleon cannon under that tent you're wearing."

Tull snatched at the buttons on his canvas coat, ripped the garment off, and slammed it onto the gritty floor. His hat followed. He held his arms out to his sides then said, "Go on. Get whatever humiliatin' shit you've got in mind over with so I can git on back there and see my wrongly incarcerated boy."

Longarm stepped up behind the quaking cattleman, lifted the heavy Remington pistol from the holster on Tull's hip, and dropped it on the desk with a reverberating *thump*. He ran his hands down each arm, along the man's rib cage, outside, then inside, each leg, and eventually stopped at the top of one boot.

"What's that?" he asked, and tapped the hard lump behind the leather.

"What's what?"

"That," Longarm said and slapped the lump even harder.

"Oh, that. Well, ain't nothin' more'n a little ole two-barreled derringer. Nothin' real important."

"Give it up," Longarm said and held out an empty hand for the weapon.

Tull angrily fished the tiny over-and-under popper out of his boot, sneered at Longarm's hand, and pitched the pistol onto the desk. "Happy now, you law-bringin', badge-totin' bastard?"

Longarm smiled at the man's effort to bait him and leaned against the desk. "He's clean, Judge. Shouldn't be a problem unless he can cut through iron bars with bullshit."

Cain snorted, then stifled a laugh by covering his mouth with a trembling hand. He turned to the deputy and said, "You can let him in now, Nate. Fifteen minutes, that's all he's got."

The deputy fished a ring of keys from the top drawer of the desk and hustled over to the door that led to the cell block. A resonant metallic *crunch* followed as he twisted the key and snapped the bolt back. "This way, sir," he said, then stepped aside as the iron-framed slab door swung open.

"Can I have my coat back now?" Tull grumped.

Longarm grabbed the garment off the floor and patted it down. He pitched it to Tull, then snatched the man's hat up off the floor. "Want this, too?" he said.

Tull slid into his coat, then angrily grabbed the hat and stuffed it back on his head. "Well, can I go back and see my son, now? Or do you want me to drop my pants and bend over so you can look up my asshole? Hell, I might be a carryin' a hacksaw blade, twelve-inch bowie knife,

or a sawed-off shotgun in there somewheres. Not kiddin'
now. Might wanna take a quick peek, fellers."

"Go visit your son, Mr. Tull," Longarm said. "You're
just wasting our time now. Trust me when I say that nobody here wants to see your old, puckered asshole."

Rufus Tull threw up his hands, slapped them back
down against his thighs, then stomped off into the cell
block.

"Should I go with him, Judge?" the deputy asked.

Cain shook his head. "That won't be necessary, Nate.
We've probably made him mad enough for one night as it
is. Bronson's the only prisoner back there right now, so it
shouldn't be a problem."

Longram dragged one of several available ladder-
backed chairs over next to the stove and took a seat. The
potbelly's glowing warmth proved a comfort after the
chilling walk. He lit a cheroot, then, to the deputy said,
"Got a mighty fine fire here, Nate. Sure feels good on a
night like this one. Appears Mother Nature's working
herself into a chilly one."

The deputy dipped his head, then said, "Glad you noticed, Marshal. Quite a job just keepin' two stoves goin'
'round here. Have to really work at it, you know. Been
keepin' 'em damped down so they won't use up so much
firewood. 'Course that feller in the back don't like it
much."

Judge Cain perked up and listened more intently when
Longarm said, "What's his particular problem?"

Nate edged closer to his guest. "Says he's cold all the
time. It really ain't all that chilly back there, Marshal.
Leastways it ain't no frostier'n it is out here. Got him in
the cell closest to the stove, and he still gripes evertime I

go back there." He glanced at the open cell block door and shook his head. "Mean, I know it's pretty nippy back yonder, early in the mornin', 'fore I can git here and git everthang goin' again. But we give him enough blankets to cover up an elephant. Bellyachin'est human I've run acrost since I took this job."

"Just have to ignore him, son," Longarm offered. "Been my experience all you have to do is lock a man up for a spell to turn him into a semiprofessional grumbler. Most of them are working under the erroneous belief that the banging gate gets a new latch."

Rufus Tull stomped back into the room and immediately lit into the deputy. "My son looks awful. 'Pears to me like the boy's on death's door. Says he's a freezin' his gonads off back there. Ain't gettin' fed right, neither. What the hell you been doin', boy? You just sittin' 'round here on your dead ass watchin' my son dry up and blow away in this never-endin' panhandle wind?"

A look of instant offense hit Deputy Nate Brice's face. "There ain't a word of what you just said got any truth in it, mister. He gits fed three times a day. My mother cooks the food for 'im. Spend most of my wakin' hours stokin' that stove back yonder 'cause he bitches constantly." The longer the boy talked the angrier and more animated he got. "Personally, I think the murderin' son of a bitch has a tapeworm the size of a Brazos riverboat and as long as the reins on a forty-mule team."

Hot blood rushed up Tull's neck and set his ears aflame. He shook a knotted finger in the young deputy's face. "You gotta lotta nerve talkin' to me with such a disrespectful tone of voice, whistle britches. Just might have to take you over my knee and switch your bony ass 'fore this whole dance is over."

Deputy Brice glanced from Longarm to Judge Cain and back again, then bowed up and snapped, "You might well be bigger, uglier, and meaner, old man, but," he patted the pistol on his hip, "I'm younger, faster, and deadlier. Don't go tryin' me."

Rufus Tull stepped back as though he'd been slapped across the face with a wet bar rag. He turned and made for the desk. "Gimme my pistol," he yelped. "I'll settle this chicken wrangler's hash right this instant."

Longarm jumped between the two angry roosters. "Need to calm down a mite, both of you. Nate, you go have a seat and get a handle on yourself. Tull, think it's time for you to collect your belongings and hit the street."

Brice immediately did as he was told and sullenly flopped into his chair behind the desk. Rufus Tull wouldn't let it go. "Ain't no man gonna run off at the mouth like that at me. Even if he is still suckin' on the tit and wearin' shit-filled didies."

Judge Cain jumped in with, "That's enough, Rufus. Everybody here knows what a bad man you are. So, do as the marshal says. Collect your accoutrement, go outside, and cool the hell off."

Longarm, the judge, and Deputy Nate Brice followed Rufus Tull into the near totally darkened street, stood in the pool of kerosene lamplight falling from the door, and watched as he angrily holstered the Remington pistol, snatched at the front of his jacket a time or two, and resettled his hat. Finally he turned, shook his finger at the freckle-faced lawman, and shouted, "This here ain't nowhere near the end of our dispute, boy. We're gonna dance a hot jig 'fore this goddamned deal all shakes out."

From somewhere across McMasters Street, and behind a stand of trees near Tascosa's courthouse, two thunderous blasts delivered a blistering shower of shot that rippled through the midst of the bubbling argument. A rush of lead pellets peppered the county building's stone wall, pocked the wooden door, and sent everyone in the group in a headlong dive for cover.

Rufus Tull yelped and disappeared into the night like he'd been taken away on a cloud of windblown dust. Deputy Nate Brice let out a surprised screech and fell back through the still open doorway he'd only recently exited.

Dirt clods, wood splinters, and stinging rock fragments filled the air in a cloudlike spray. The booming barrage of gunfire echoed up and down Tascosa's streets and set dogs to barking and howling all over the north end of town. The acrid smell of burnt black-powder, singed cloth, and fresh blood drifted across McMasters Street. Then, for a few seconds, an unsettling quiet dropped down on the entire scene as though skeletal death's moldered, rotting raiments had been draped over a cold, dark world.

Chapter 7

Longarm landed awkwardly and hard on his stomach behind the water trough only a few steps from the Oldham
County Jail's front entrance. He grunted, rolled to one
side, then pulled his pistol. Shocked, and a bit surprised
by the explosive turn of events, he ripped the hat from his
head and tried to sneak a peek over the side of the trough.
Squinting hard, he found it impossible to pierce the blue-
black darkness of the moonless, cloudy night. The light
from the open doorway helped further obscure what little
he could see.

"Who's hit? Anybody hit?" he called out.

"Me for one, goddammit. Backshootin' bastard put
burnin' lead in my hide," Rufus Tull yelped. "Sprayed me
all up and down my right leg."

From inside the county building, Nate Brice's voice
quivered as he shouted, "Shit, Marshal. Think I got some
of it, too. Good God, I'm bleedin' from spots all over my
side."

Longarm popped up, threw a hasty glance around in
an effort to spot Rufus Tull, then ducked back down.
"Where in the hell are you, Rufus?"

A second of silence passed, then he heard the tougher-than-a-hog's-snout rancher cough, spit, and throw curses at heaven directed at an unthinking God. "I made it to the scrawny-assed live oak over to your right, Marshal. Doubt you can see me here in the dark. 'Pears I'm pretty well sheltered, for the time being. Leastways, figure I'm okay if'n I don't move 'round much."

"Well, then, don't move around. We've got light behind us. Made damned fine targets silhouetted in the dark the way we were," Longarm yelled.

Two more ear-shattering, rapid-fire blasts lit the inky night and seemed to splatter everything for ten feet in all directions around Longarm's hastily chosen hiding place. "Damn," he muttered and scrunched down as low as he could. "There's one helluva spread on that thing. Sounds like a sawed-off ten-gauge."

After another period of ear-straining quiet, he rolled onto his back and struggled to hear anything at all in the way of movement. Seconds dragged into what felt like minutes. Minutes crawled past like hours. An artificial eternity with no additional gunfire passed.

From inside the county's brand-new building, Judge Cain called out, "Think whoever did the shooting might be gone now, Marshal. If you can get inside safely, we are in need of your assistance. I fear Deputy Brice could well be seriously wounded."

Longarm squirmed around on the ground and glanced back through the still open doorway. "For the love of God, Judge, put that lamp out 'til I can get inside."

Seconds later the light finally died. The entire area around the entrance on McMaster's Street was plunged into total, can't-see-your-hand-in-front-of-your-face darkness. Barking animals from all corners of town settled into low, grumbling yaps and snarls.

Longarm holstered the pistol and rolled onto his hands and knees. He stayed as low as he could, crawfished back inside the Oldham County Jail, then pushed the heavy door closed with his foot. "You can relight the lamp now, Judge," he said as he rose to his knees.

A sulfur match flared up in Judge Henry Cain's shaking hand. A few seconds later, the wick of a kerosene lantern flickered to sputtering life. The reddish-orange flame cast a feeble, tremulous pool of light on the bloody situation.

Nate Brice lay on the floor, wide-eyed and motionless, his back propped against the sheriff's new desk. Longarm gazed down at the wounded man and shook his head. Tiny, still-smoking, holes—their edges tinged black from superheated shot—decorated one side of the terrified deputy's faded bib-front shirt, and the leg of his plaid woolen pants.

Brice made a frightened kind of half-pawing, half-pointing motion at the shot-riddled spot on his side, but didn't touch it. He cast a wide-eyed glance at Longarm and muttered, "How bad am I hurt, Marshal? Can you see? Say somethin'. Ain't gonna die, am I?"

Longarm shook his head. "I can't detect any real damage on the surface, Nate. To tell the absolute truth, son, right now it don't look too bad at all."

"You sure?"

"Them's some tiny little holes. Appears whoever was doing the blasting might have used bird shot on us. But, hell, that just don't make any sense. It's near a hundred feet over to the courthouse where the shootin' came from.

A man can't do much damage with that light a load from such a distance. If I was gonna ambush somebody, wouldn't load up with nothin' but buckshot for the job. Make sure I put 'em down right quick."

Judge Cain stepped over and held the lamp closer to the deputy's wounds. "Bird shot makes absolutely perfect sense to me, Marshal."

Longram leaned back on his heels. "How so, Judge?"

Cain threw quick, nervous glances at the door as though expecting red-eyed death to break in and step across the threshold at any moment. "I think whoever fired on us merely wanted to send a rather pointed message," he said, as he glared at Longarm through the dancing, blood-colored lamplight.

"And what message might that be, in your learned estimation, Judge?" Longarm didn't wait for an answer. He pulled a folding knife from his vest pocket and cut the cloth away from Nate Brice's body. "Try not to move, son. I wouldn't want to put any more holes in you than you've already got."

"Shit," Brice said, "this here's my best shirt. Couldn't you just pull the tail up outta my pants?"

Longarm shook his head. "Probably best to do it this way. Don't want to disturb the wound any more than necessary, leastways until we can get a good look and determine just how bad you're hit."

"Don't really hurt all that much," Brice mumbled as though talking to himself. "Just burns like a son of a bitch. Kinda like when you get a splinter in your finger, you know?"

"I've seen men gut shot who didn't feel a thing immediately after gettin' hit, Nate," Longarm said and continued to hack away at the shirt. "You just hang on for a few more seconds."

A grim tinge of fear rattled in Judge Henry Cain's tremulous, detached voice as he said, " 'I can kill you anytime I want.' That was the message, Marshal. Plain as a cold, clear day in Amarillo. 'I can kill you anytime I want.' That's what the assassin was saying to us."

"Well, maybe, Judge, maybe," Longarm said, then lifted the chewed-up material of Brice's shirt away and gazed at the reddish, spotted wound on the boy's side. A smile creaked across his face and he nodded. "Well, you got dusted pretty good, Nate. But, looks to me like the twenty or so pieces of shot here barely managed to punch through your shirt. Most of 'em are just kinda sitting there under your skin like hard black bubbles. Doubt those as hit your leg even got through your pants. Looks like luck was with you tonight, son."

He probed some of the blood-encircled BBs under Brice's skin with the tip of his finger. One popped out and washed away in a tiny stream of scarlet. "Shouldn't be much of a problem gettin' 'em out, Nate. Come on, now, let me help you up."

Brice wobbled to unsteady feet and began his own wide-eyed examination of the leaking wound that ran from midway of his chest to the waist of his woolen pants. "Damnation. I ain't never been shot before, fellers. Surprised me so, I didn't even know what to think when I got hit." He glanced at the two men. "Damned things burned like hornet stings, or scorpion bites. Some of 'em still do."

From the cell block, Tascosa's only prisoner yelled, "What in the blue-eyed hell's a goin' on out there? Can anybody hear me? Pa, are you out there?"

Cain strode to the cell block door and snatched open the tiny window used to check on prisoners. "Hold your water a bit longer, Bronson. We've got something of a crisis out here right now."

"Crisis? What kinda crisis, Judge? Thought I heard shootin'. Somebody done been shot? Was my pa the one what got shot? Come on now. Somebody answer me."

"We'll be with you as soon as we can," Cain yelled back through the hand-sized aperture.

The front door burst open and crashed against the wall with a loud *thud*. All three men made a hasty grab for their pistols. Cocked Remington still firmly in hand, Rufus Tull stumbled over the threshold and dropped to the floor, then scrambled to a spot where he could sit with his back against the wall. "Out yonder under that tree, I got to thinkin' as how you law-bringin' sons of bitches was just gonna let me lay out there in the dark and fuckin' bleed to death," he croaked.

Longarm turned, grabbed the door, and flung it shut. "Sorry, Rufus, I hadn't forgot about you, but we had our hands full in here."

Cain added, "Honestly, we didn't mean to ignore you."

"So you bastards both say," Tull grunted. "Probably in here a sendin' up prayers and a hopin' I'd done passed on for a hot greetin' on Satan's front door step."

"That's a steamin' pile of horseshit, mister," Nate Brice snapped. "They were helpin' me. Thank God, I ain't hurt as bad as first appearances would have indicated."

"How is it with you, Rufus?" Judge Cain asked as he raised the kerosene lamp higher in an effort to get a better light on the situation.

Tull glared at Brice, then leaned over as far as he could and gazed down at his blood-soaked pant leg. "Hell, boys, cain't really tell myself. Know I'm hit down there 'round my knee somewheres. But it was too damned dark out in the street to see how much damage that ambushin' piece of skunk shit did. Does hurt a mite, though."

Longarm moved to Tull's side and went to hacking at the damaged, blood-spattered area of the man's chaps and woolen britches. He pulled the perforated material aside to reveal several puncture wounds similar to those in the deputy's side. "Most of the blast didn't do any more real damage than those that hit Nate," Longarm said. "But there's at least two or three pieces of the shot that went in considerably deeper. Looks like the majority of 'em got you on the back of your leg. You must have been in the act of turning around when you got hit."

Tull grimaced and squirmed against the wall. "Well, somethin' down there hurts a lot worse than the others."

Longarm poked at a spot on the man's bleeding leg. "Does appear kind of like you might have one piece lodged behind the kneecap. Gonna be hard to the point of impossible to get it out, I'll bet."

Tull reached down and slapped the ragged piece of material back over the still oozing wounds. "Shit, I've been hurt a helluva lot worse than this, more times than I care to remember. Yankee sniper got me with a through and through in the thigh of my other leg durin' Mr. Lincoln's war of Yankee aggression agin' the South. Whoopin' Comanche shot an arrow into my guts back in sixty-nine. I'm still carryin' a good-sized piece of the flint head. Hell, I've got battle scars all over my body, Long. Gimme a couple a days' rest. I'll be good as new."

Longarm wiped the bloody knife blade off with a kerchief, snapped it shut, placed both back in his pocket, then locked Tull in a hard gaze. "You're in need of a doctor's attention, Rufus. If either one of those wounds gets infected, you could lose that leg."

"He's right, Rufus. Just about all of Deputy Brice's wounds appear superficial. You've got some places on that leg that look pretty bad to me," Judge Cain added.

Nate Brice glanced up from his own injuries. "We ain't got no doc in Tascosa, gents."

Rufus Tull wagged his head like a tired dog. "Ain't got no doctor? What the hell kinda backward, out-of-the-way, pissant-sized town is this? Might as well be livin' on the trail with a bunch of ignert damned brush-poppin' waddies and crazier'n'hell longhorns."

Brice shook his head. "Feller down at the drugstore might be able to help some. But, still and all, he ain't no doc. Sorry to be the one to break the bad news to you fellers."

Longarm stood. He continued to stare down at Tull's damaged leg. "Well, there's always a chance nothing will come of it. If you're lucky, the body'll just cover up the various intrusions and that'll be the end of the whole deal. I just wanted to make you aware of the possibility for a less than positive outcome."

"While some might say I look it, I ain't exactly dumber'n a wagonload of rocks, Marshal," Tull grumped. "Know exactly what the possibilities are, for the love of sweet weepin' Christ. Now, stop jawin' around, find me some whiskey, and let's get this mess cleaned up."

Brice pointed at the desk and said, "They's a near full bottle of hundred-fifty-proof panther sweat in the bottom drawer yonder. Stuff's potent enough to kill damned near anything you've got. Sheriff Best keeps it here for just such needs. Whatever you do, though, don't get any of the damned stuff on your clothes—it'll eat right through.

After nearly thirty minutes of blood-saturated effort, Longarm and Judge Cain had done about as much as they could to repair the injuries inflicted on both men. Tull's wounds were cleansed and bandaged, and as much of the shot picked from the raw skin of Deputy Brice's side as possible.

A sizable crowd of gawkers, drawn to the scene by the gunfire, had gathered outside the jail and buzzed like a nest of angry hornets. Brice stepped into the street and tried to explain the unsettling set of recent events to the inquisitive, the inebriated, and the semi-inebriated.

Tull gave up his pistol again and hobbled back into the cell block to speak with his son. For a few minutes, Judge Cain and Longarm were left alone in the office.

Cain paced back and forth like a caged animal, while Longarm stood at a basin of water and cleansed his bloody hands.

"I'm most distressed by all this," Cain said. "Most distressed."

"Well, I don't think you can be a whole lot more *distressed* than I am," Longarm replied.

Cain stopped his pacing, but appeared to tremble all over like a man in the final life-stealing throes of a vicious attack of malaria. He shook a quivering, manicured finger at Longarm. "I sent for you in particular, Marshal Long, because I had every reason to fear exactly this kind of outcome given the previous threats made against my life. Figured a man of your reputation would provide me with exactly the kind of security I needed. This bloody episode tonight has most assuredly shaken that faith."

Towel in hand, Longarm turned on Cain and said, "Threatening a man's life is one thing, Judge. Actually trying to make good on the threat is an entirely different animal altogether. Hell, any man who's been in the law as long as you knows that better than me. People who've worked at this game as long as we have understand there's a world chockful of big behavers, blowhards, wind-bellys, and flannel-mouths. Hell's eternal bells, we live in a world full of jackasses who're given to spoutin' off anytime they have half a fuckin' chance. But ninety-nine percent of the time, they never carry through on their bullyin' blatheration."

Cain's voice betrayed a deepening agitation when he shot back, "That's not what happened here, by God. Someone hid out there in the dark tonight. Sent a very clear message of just how easy it would be to take my life, yours, or anyone else's who might get in their way. To be perfectly blunt, Marshal Long, and as I said before, my confidence in your ability to protect me from harm has suffered greatly as a consequence of what occurred out there in McMasters Street this very evening."

Longarm pitched the soiled, bloodstained towel aside and pushed the sleeves of his shirt back down, then retrieved his coat and slid into it. "Look, Judge," he said as he ran his fingers through disheveled hair, "I'm a ways from being persuaded that the most accomplished gunman on this earth could absolutely ensure your complete safety, or anyone else's for that matter, from a determined, well-armed killer. Given the absolute certainty of such a reality, what in the blue-eyed hell would you have me do? Go on, tell me."

Several seconds of chin-scratching silence followed. Cain paced back and forth from the desk to the cell block door. Of a sudden he stopped dead in his tracks and stared at the floor. As though talking to himself, or perhaps the dusty boards in the rough floor, he said, "Don't know why I didn't think of this before. By far the most logical solution for the entire problem." He glanced up at Longarm, nodded and said, "Yes, that's exactly what we'll do."

"Well, are you gonna let me in on this revelation, or do I have to lay hands on your skull and hope for divine deliverance of the plan through my fingertips?"

Cain smiled at Longarm as though gazing at a testy child. "We'll move into the jail. Stone building, iron bars, heavy doors. Without doubt it's by far the safest place in town. Yep, that's the ticket all right. We'll just stay here until Bronson Tull's trial is over, and I've sentenced him to hang by the neck until dead, dead, dead."

Chapter 8

Longarm stared at Henry Cain in bemused silence for several seconds, then said, "Move into the jail, huh? You pullin' my leg here, Judge? Are you serious?"

"Dead serious," Cain snapped. "County has plenty of empty beds back there in the cell block. Five, as a matter of pure fact. Courthouse is right across the street—less than fifty paces. Whole proposition will be a lot more convenient—and a hell of a lot safer—for us to reside here, rather than walk back and forth from the hotel and chance another ambush with every trip along the way."

"While all that's true, Judge, you'll very likely have to limit your movements outside these walls, no matter what we do."

Cain waved the lawman's logical assessment away as though it amounted to nothing more than a troublesome blowfly. "Doesn't matter. Not one whit. If I push it, the trial shouldn't last any more than two, maybe three days at the absolute longest. Bronson Tull's guiltier than dangling Judas. The Amarillo prosecutor has a dozen subpoenaed witnesses he's bringing up who saw the killing. Those fine folk stand ready and eager to testify to his culpability in this matter. A jury of Tull's peers will find exactly as I expect; then I can sentence the homicidal skunk to hang and get on back home to my wife and family."

Longarm shook his head. "What exactly makes you think you'll be safe once the trial ends, Judge? Especially if Tull's found guilty? Or that these walls will keep anything wayward from happening to us during the course of the trial?"

Cain leaned closer, and in a rasping whisper said, "Look, Marshal Long, we both know Rufus Tull is behind tonight's whole misbegotten mess. The wicked old son of a bitch is determined to keep his lowlife, murderous, scum-sucking son out of a cold-eyed executioner's life-stealing grasp."

"I'm not so sure, Judge."

"Well, I am. And I'm convinced he's more than a little bit willing to see me dead to do it. In fact, now that I've given a bit of thought to the whole affair, I'd bet my Palo Duro Canyon ranch, ole Rufus wrote every one of those bullying notes I showed you earlier."

Longarm threw up his hands, then let them flop to his sides. "Jesus, Judge, if that's true, why was he the one who got shot tonight? Do you actually think he'd have his own man shoot him down in the street like a yellow dog?"

A huge smile spread over Cain's masklike face. "Hell yes. The man's despicably evil through and through. Rufus Tull's a nefarious snake that I wouldn't trust any farther than I could throw a burlap bag full of freshly forged anvils. Getting peppered with a little bird shot goes a long way to making us think otherwise—takes our concentrated attention off the immediate problem at hand. Quite the clever plan when you give the thing any thought at all."

"Well, that's just damned ridiculous. If what happened out in the street tonight proves anything to me, it's that Rufus Tull didn't have shit to do with it."

Cain's head snapped back as though he'd been slapped. "How on earth could you have arrived at such an erroneous and poorly reasoned conclusion?"

"Because, ole Rufus might be rougher 'n a cob, and a serious case of hell on wheels when it comes to preserving the life of one of the only two sons he has left. But, I'll just be damned if I'll ever be able to believe he's smart enough to hire someone to shoot him down out front of Tascosa's jailhouse in a calculated move to make us believe a set of circumstances that are patently unthinkable."

Cain's eyes bugged, and he swelled up like a south Texas horned toad. "I'm not going to debate this any further with you, Marshal Long." He pulled a key from his coat pocket and pitched it at the surprised lawman. "Get over to the Exchange Hotel and bring all my belongings back here. I'll be staying in one of the cells until such time as Bronson Tull's trial ends and the man is duly and legally sentenced to hang. That's my final decision, and I'm sticking to it."

"What about me?"

Cain strode to the sheriff's desk and leaned against it. He struck a thoughtful pose, then said, "You can do as you please, except at those times when I need you to escort me back and forth to the courthouse."

"Do as I please?"

"Well, within certain limits."

"What the hell does that mean? What limits?"

Cain went back to scratching his chin again before saying, "To begin with, I think it might be wise for you to deputize at least two more men to assist in protecting my person."

"Deputize two more men? Where am I to get two more men?"

"I don't care where you get them. If I didn't learn another thing from tonight's dustup, I was impressed with the overall need for a larger cadre of federal officers to accompany me at all times. With Sheriff Best out of town, his only deputy wounded, and a question mark when it comes to applying himself to his regular duties, there's the possibility you might well have to assume some of his responsibilities as well. Additionally, I will insist on personal protection daylight and dark until this situation comes to an end."

Longarm's neck and ears reddened. "You expect me to assume the responsibilities of Deputy Brice and try to keep you alive at the same time?"

"If necessary, yes. Absolutely."

On the verge of purple-faced rage, Longarm snapped, "Now, just what the hell does that mean?"

"Exactly as I said."

Longarm snatched his hat off the peg over the wash basin and stuffed it back on his head. "I'm a deputy U.S. marshal, Judge, and don't have a problem with any duties pursuant to my commission, as outlined by the federal government and my immediate supervisor, Marshal Billy Vail. However, I do not feel that arresting town drunks, herding crooked gamblers, supervising soiled doves, cleaning up horse shit, running pigs out of the alleyways, and patrolling the streets of a half-assed burg like Tascosa for whoop-and-holler cowboys are included in that commission."

Cain brought himself erect as though an iron rod had been suddenly inserted into his spine. "You, sir, are here at my request, and under my supervision. You will damn well do as I order. Either that, or I'm just about certain a telegraphed message to the U.S. Marshal's Office in Denver will ensure your compliance."

Two quick steps brought Longarm and Cain almost nose to nose. In what amounted to a threatening growl, Longarm snarled, "I'm bound by my own personal sense of duty and commitment to do everything in my power to see to your safety, Judge. But don't, for one single second, entertain the erroneous thought that I'll perform like some organ grinder's monkey on a leather string just because some unknown jackass with a shotgun jammed a burr up your butt."

Cain's eyes narrowed and his lips twitched. "We now know beyond any doubt that our lives are in danger, Marshal Long. I expect you to perform all duties as required by the circumstances, *and as I deem necessary by unexpected changes in those circumstances*."

Longarm twirled on his heel and stomped back into the street. He stopped just outside the door, angrily scratched a sulfur match to life on the butt of his pistol, and lit a cheroot.

Deputy Nate Brice had shooed most of the gawkers out of the street. With an arm tenderly clutched against his wounded side, he hobbled back toward the jail and stopped a few feet from where Longarm stood. Light from the doorway fell on the boy's pained expression.

"Think they're all gone now, Marshal. Just a bunch of curious drunks that heard the commotion."

Longarm glanced at the boy and noted his discomfort. "How're you feelin', Nate?"

Brice looked away and cast a weary glance down Mc-Masters Street toward Main, where lights still burned in most of the saloons and gambling establishments. "Well, I have to admit, I ain't at my best, right now, Marshal

Long. Sure would help if I could put my head down for a spell. Be a blessing to get home and tell my wife 'bout all this 'fore she hears somethin' from some idiot that don't know what he's talkin' about that'll just upset her."

"You're married?"

"Yessir. Got hitched a couple of months ago. Mexican gal. Maria Conchita Esparza Brice. She's a pistol. Makes the best tamales in Texas. We rent a little house over on Marby Avenue, near the St. Barnabas Catholic Church. Maria has this thing 'bout bein' as close to God as she can."

"She sounds like a real catch."

"I think so."

Longarm flicked ashes from his smoke into the street, then took another deep drag on the stogie before he said, "Look, I've got an errand to run. Me and Judge Cain are gonna move into Sheriff Best's office until this trial is over."

"You're movin' into the jail?"

"Yep. If you can stick around for about another hour, when I get back, I think you should be able to take off, go on home, and get some rest. I'll be glad to watch the jail while you're away. I might even patrol around town some while you recuperate a bit."

A deep sigh escaped Nate Brice's lips and a grinning look of relief washed over his pale, pain-pinched face. He gingerly rubbed the wounded spot on his side. "You'd do that for me, Marshal?"

Longarm raised his hand to slap the boy on his good shoulder, thought better of it, and just gave him a friendly pat on the back. "Sure. You go have a seat in there next to the stove. I'll be back just as quick as I can."

"Thanks, Marshal. You can't imagine how much I appreciate all this. Thought sure I was just gonna have to stick around here and suffer. Sheriff Best said I shouldn't leave the prisoner alone, you know."

"Don't worry about the prisoner. I'll take care of him," Longarm said, then turned and heeled it for the Exchange Hotel.

"Thanks again, Marshal," the boy called at Longarm's disappearing back.

Every building, tree, fence post, and bush along the murky, abandoned thoroughfare now cast ominous, shimmering apparitions across the still angry lawdog's path. He resettled his pistol belt, then tickled the grip of the Frontier model Colt, as he picked a cautious path toward Tascosa's central business district. He drew into the darkest shadows on the west side of the street and stopped several times with an ear cocked for anything in the way of threatening movement.

At the corner of McMasters, he paused and peered as far as he could along the dimly lit avenue that led to the hotel, then turned and headed west along Main. Pale flickers of lamplight filtered through an ever-present cloud of hanging dust and cascaded from windows and doorways the entire length of the still active street.

He'd barely made it past the false front of James McMasters's combination grocery emporium and post office, when a group of six or eight boisterous cowboys erupted out of the darkness and whipped their ponies along the street in a tempest of flying dust, dirt clods, whoops, and hollers.

Taken aback by the sudden blast of racket and turmoil, Longarm pressed himself against the wall of Wright and Farnsworth's General store. The hooting, hat-waving crew of brush-poppers vanished, as suddenly as they appeared, and the wagon-rutted main thoroughfare went nearly silent once again. Other than the occasional intrusion of rowdy voices and raucous laughter coming from the open doorways of several still open saloons and restaurants, there was almost no movement or other sounds intruding on the deathly still night.

As Longarm made his way through the Exchange Hotel's lobby and past the desk, he noticed a new clerk. "Where's that other feller? Chauncy Pedigrew?"

Oily, bald, thin as a mashed snake, and sporting an enormous handlebar moustache, the desk clerk offered up an insincere smile, then said, "Day man. I'm the night man. Chauncy gets off every afternoon around six. Be more than happy to help you if I can, sir."

"Well, Night Man, my name's Custis Long—Deputy U.S. Marshal Custis Long. You can check Judge Henry Cain and me out. Recent events have forced us to move all our operations into Sheriff Jim Best's over at the Oldham County Jail facilities."

"I see," the expressionless clerk sniffed.

Longarm glanced around the lobby, then said, "Chauncy said you had a boy who stayed on call for errands."

"Yes. That is true. Name's Jesse Perkins."

Longarm dropped a silver dollar on the front desk. "Send him to my room. If I'm not there, tell him to look next door. May need his assistance moving our belongings."

"He'll be there shortly, sir," the clerk called to the departing marshal's back, then slipped the heavy coin into his vest pocket.

As he'd not had a chance to unpack when he arrived, the job of gathering up his own belongings took Longarm only a few seconds. Everything he'd handed over to

Chauncy Pedigrew earlier that afternoon was still arranged in a neat pile in the middle of a freshly made bed. He poked around in the stack for a moment in an effort to make sure everything was in order, then decided to leave all his trappings as they were, strode to the judge's room and started to insert the key. The door creaked open on dry, brass hinges when he touched it.

Longarm backed up against the wall and pulled his pistol. He waited a long moment, then took a single wary step into the unlit room. Flickering light from kerosene lamps mounted in wooden sconces along the hallway squeezed its way around him and bounced across ever-changing areas of Henry Cain's former quarters.

Not a single recognizable stick of furniture remained in its proper place. Bedclothes, furnishings, and Judge Cain's belongings lay thrown into a single enormous pile in the middle of the floor.

The insane scene appeared as though a cyclone had gone through and left an isolated path of total destruction that resulted in a miniature mountain of splintered junk and tattered clothing. A wicked, skin-prickling sound jittered from dark corners and beneath the newly created mountain of clutter.

Longarm eyeballed the dark corners of the room and then took another cautious step inside.

"Sweet sufferin' Jesus," yelped a high-pitched voice.

Ready to deal bloody death, Longarm whirled. A dirty-faced urchin of about twelve or thirteen stood nose to gun barrel and blinked long-lashed eyes. He appeared more in awe than scared. "Name's Jesse Perkins," the boy boldly offered. He placed a grubby finger atop Long's pistol barrel and eased it off to one side, then hooked a thumb back down the hall toward the desk. "Baldheaded son of a bitch out front woke me the fuck up and says you might be a needin' a mite of help, mister."

Longarm cast a quick, mildly irritated glance at the kid, then eased back around and went on with his inch-by-inch, scanning search of the ravaged room. "From the looks of things, I might well require more than a 'little help,' 'fore this night's over, Jesse."

Perkins moved up next to Longarm, snatched a tattered, gray-felt cap from his unkept head and peeked around the stock-still marshal at the jumbled confusion inside the room. "Sweet sufferin' Jesus," he said. "When that walkin' asshole, Chauncy Pedigrew, sees this disaster, he's gonna drop a log the size of a yellow-meat watermelon. Man just don't take kindly to them folk as would have nerve enough to make a mess of the rooms. And, you gotta admit, mister, you done gone and made one helluva fuckin' mess."

Longarm slid his pistol back into its holster, but made no move to go any deeper into the room. "It's a real sow's nest all right," he mumbled and continued his squint-eyed examination. Then, in what seemed an afterthought, he calmly added, "You know, Jesse, for a youngster of such tender years, you've got one astonishingly filthy mouth on you."

The stray threw his head back and cackled. "Now's that a fuckin' fact."

"Exactly my sentiments as well."

"What can I say? I'm the sorry product of a broken home and a piss-poor raisin' that took place mainly around saloons and whorehouses. Oh, and by the way, you're pretty damned ugly, mister. Hell, never knowed nobody what bothered to stack horse shit as tall as you are. Guess I'm fated to learn somethin' horrible every fuckin' day 'bout tall, strange, ugly cocksuckers who have a thing about destroyin' hotel rooms."

Longarm turned and shook a finger in the scamp's face. Jesse Perkins twisted the floppy cap around in his hands, then cocked his dirty head to one side like an inquisitive dog that'd just happened on its first porcupine. "You hear that? What the bloody hell's that buzzin' noise, mister? Makes the skin on my back pimple up."

"Snakes, I think. Lots of snakes."

Perkins took a step backward into the hallway. "Snakes? Shit and damnation, but I hate snakes. All of 'em. Every kind, shape, color, and scale-covered description. Tongue-flickin' sons of bitches give me the chicken-fleshed willies jus' thinkin' 'bout 'em."

In spite of himself, Longarm grinned at the boy. "Rattlers, Jesse, my fine-talkin', likely-to-be-a-Bible-thumpin'-evangelist friend. And if the sound they're makin' is any indication of size, they're big ones."

The scruffy waif lolled his head over to one side again and sniffed. "You smell somethin' like meadow muffins a-burnin', mister?"

Longarm flared his nostrils and sampled the stale air. "Now that you mention it, yes, I do. Familiar, but can't quite . . . Tryin' to figure out what it is and where it's coming . . . Damned if that don't smell . . . Good God Almighty, I don't believe . . ."

Longarm turned, took a single step, dove through the doorway, grabbed the kid on his way down, and jerked the surprised boy to the floor. A thunderous explosion slapped them both hard across their backs. A wave of pressure from burnt black powder blew bedclothing, pieces of wooden furniture, snakes, bits of snakes, splinters from the door facing, most of the door, and chunks of the ceiling into the narrow hallway.

The churning wave surged toward the hotel lobby in a blurred swirl of smoke, dust, and floating pieces of rendered cloth and paper. A dirty, gray cloud engulfed everything in its path, snuffed all the hallway lamps, and turned the entire world as black as a windowless, corner closet in Satan's basement. When Longarm finally wobbled back to his feet, the kid had disappeared like spit on a hot stove lid.

Chapter 9

Judge Henry Cain stood just inside his shattered hotel room. He gazed at the destruction in trembling, dumbfounded amazement. "Jesus H. Christ," he sputtered. "Still don't believe this. We heard the explosion all the way over at the jail. I just knew something like this had happened. Just damned knew it."

Longarm leaned against the splintered door frame and slapped his hat against a dust-covered leg. As he picked wood splinters out of his suit jacket, he said, "Notice anything particularly odd about the damage, Judge?"

Cain swayed around to face his bodyguard. "Odd? What the hell does that mean?"

"Odd. You know, out of the ordinary. Strange. Peculiar."

Cain snatched up what appeared to be part of a now destroyed pair of men's pants. "I know what the word means, goddammit. Mere fact that anyone had nerve enough to pull a stunt like this strikes me as damned odd. What I don't know is what you meant by such an infernally dimwitted question, Marshal Long."

Longarm fought back an overwhelming urge to slap the man's face till his nose bled and thereby snap him out of unreasoning hysterics. Instead he calmed himself, and, in as reasonable a tone as he could muster, said, "Take another look around, Judge. I think you might be missing something just a shade on the important side."

Cain motioned from wall to wall with his hat, then slapped his leg with it in disgust. "Nothing. No. Can't see it. Just one helluva mess. What on God's green earth are you talking about?" he snapped.

"Well, it would seem to me," Longarm said as though talking to a small child, "if whoever planted this bomb wanted you or me dead, the resulting explosion would have done a damned sight more serious damage than we see here. No doubt about it, the result is a glowing testament to what gunpowder can do. But, look Judge, this pile of debris ain't nothin' near what could have resulted from the application of just a bit more explosive power."

"Sweet sufferin' Savior, how much more destruction do you want, Long? The damned explosion rendered everything in the room to nothing more than a pile of dust, destroyed clothing, and worthless junk."

Longarm pulled a cheroot from his vest pocket, then took his own sweet time lighting it. Shook the match to death and thumped it onto the still smoldering pile of rubble in the middle of the floor. "True, but the walls are still standing. Blast for damned sure made a lot of racket. Might have even torn everything in the room to pieces times ten, including half a dozen rattlesnakes. But, for all that, the explosion barely managed to knock the window out. Most of the force went out the door, down the hall, and all the way out to the lobby."

"So? What do you mean by 'might have'?"

"Take a closer look, Judge. When I walked in here earlier this evening, everything in the room was in a single pile. The clothing, sheets, towels, pillowcases, and such like could have already been rendered into bits before the detonation occurred. Didn't have time to get a good look at what was really here. Truth is, I think this whole incident doesn't amount to any more than the phony bird shot ambush down by the jail."

Cain's face reddened. He trembled from foot to crown again. "A man would need considerable experience with explosives to pull off a stunt like this and, at the same time, be able to minimize the damage to nothing more than a lot of noise, smoke, and a pile of shredded laundry and dead snakes in the middle of the floor."

Sucking air like someone on the verge of drowning, Jesse Perkins burst into the room. He flashed a breathless smile at Longarm and said, "I brung 'im. Done jus' like you tole me, Marshal. He's a-comin' down the hall." The boy held a grit-encrusted hand over his mouth as though to keep the wrong person from hearing. "I'd be careful, though, if'n I wuz either one a you fellers. See, he's a mite on the agitated side right now. Had to tell him all about the explosion, destruction, snakes, and such, don't you know."

Chauncy Pedigrew pushed his way past Jesse like the town rummy coming off a three-day drunk. He stopped in the doorway and slapped his forehead with a sweaty palm. "Good God Almighty. Look at this mess. It's a goddamned catastrophe, that's what it is, a catastrophe. For the sweet love of God, what am I ever gonna tell Mr. Russell?"

Longarm glanced at Perkins. The boy had a smile on

his face as wide as all outdoors. Longarm grinned, then said, "Who's Mr. Russell, Chauncy?"

Pedigrew stumbled around the room, pulled at his hair like someone on the verge of a breakdown and insanity, and said, "The owner. Built this place. Hell, it's his pride and joy. 'Course he won't be back for four to six weeks. On a trip back East. Death in the family, I think. Plus some other business on the side."

Henry Cain waved Pedigrew into silence. "Don't worry, Chauncy. Calm yourself. I'll hire some Mexicans. Have this all cleaned up tomorrow. Bit of carpentry here and there, dab of paint, and you won't even know anything happened here."

Pedigrew still had the look of a man about to pass a kidney stone the size of an armadillo. "Yeah, but who's gonna pay for it, Judge?"

"Oldham County will foot the bill for anything necessary to put this right. Let not your heart be troubled, Mr. Pedigrew. I'll take care of everything." With that, Cain turned to Longarm, shook his finger in the lawman's face, and said, "I'm going back to the jail. There's still some safety there, at least for the time being. I want those extra deputies on the job at the absolute earliest possible instant, Marshal. Whoever's responsible for the notes, the ambush, and now this mess appears to be about as serious as pneumonia."

As Cain stomped through the wreckage and vanished out the doorway, Nate Brice appeared and motioned Longarm into the hall. A degree of testiness crept into Longarm's voice when he said, "Thought I told you to go back to the jail and wait for me, Nate."

"Wuz on my way, Marshal. Stopped at the Equity for a bit of self-medication. You know, cow-country doctorin', as it were. Anyway, figured a healthy drink or two might help some with the pain."

Longarm smiled. "Well, that could well be, I suppose." He grabbed Brice by the elbow and shoved him toward the hotel lobby. "But you let me be the doctor in this case, son. Now head on home."

Brice stopped, glanced around as though fearful he might be overheard, then said, "You gotta listen for a minute, Marhsal. There's something new in the mix I thought you might like to know about."

The secretive urgency in the deputy's voice brought Longarm up short. "Yeah. And what would that be, Nate?"

In a husky whisper, Brice said, "They's some serious-lookin' gunnies just rode into town. Heard one of 'em askin' 'round about the trial, Judge Cain, and where he could find Rufus Tull."

"Where are they?"

"Like I said. Last I seen 'em, they wuz camped out at the Equity when I left a few minutes ago."

Longarm leaned closer. "Recognize any of them?"

"Yessir. As a matter of pure fact I did. Think the feller askin' all the questions wuz Duncan Swords. And, if I'm right about him, them other two wuz most likely Marion Mad Dog McCord, and Selby Boggs."

Longarm shot a quick glance down the hallway toward the lobby. A wave of hot blood rose from his feet and surged its way to his neck, causing a prickling sensation around his ears. Duncan Swords. "Jesus," he said as though to himself.

Brice clutched at the marshal's sleeve. "If there's three men carryin' worse reputations in Texas, I cain't imagine who they'd be. Sons of bitches sure 'nuff emptied the Equity out quicker'n a roadrunner on a rattler. People poured out of the place like sand bein' emptied from a boot."

Longarm stared at his feet for several seconds, then toed at the well-worn hallway carpet. "Well, can't blame 'em much, Nate. Swords and his kind are dangerous men. Men you don't want to have any trouble with. And I do mean any kind of trouble, even the most insignificant. They'll kill you soon as spit."

Brice absentmindedly picked at the place on his side where he'd been shot. "You reckon Rufus sent for 'em, Marshal? You reckon them skunks done come here to kill all us lawmen and break ole Bronson out? Hell, I've heard stories of some damned awful things them fellers have went and done in the past."

"Got no way of knowin' the answer to any of your questions right now, Nate. Just plain don't know. But you're as right as a barrel of fresh rain about Swords and his friends. The fortuitous appearance of three of Texas's most prolific killers in Tascosa at this exact moment in time has a somewhat suspicious tinge to it, don't you think?"

"Yessir. Yessir, I do at that. What you plan on doin' 'bout 'em, Marshal? Or, guess maybe I shoulda said, what do we plan on doin' 'bout 'em?"

Longarm scratched his chin, ran his hand around the back of his neck, and shook his head. "Not sure 'bout that one either, Nate. Not exactly sure yet, anyway." Then he grabbed the young deputy by the arm and escorted him down the hall, through the lobby, and into the street.

Once they'd made it outside, Longarm pushed the boy away and said, "Go on home to your wife, son. Spend a good night with her. We'll worry 'bout this tomorrow mornin'." Brice tried to object, but Longarm pushed him away and said, "Do like I told you, Nate. Go on home. I'll take care of things while you're down. Go on now. It'll be all right."

Brice bobbed his head in reluctant acceptance, then hobbled away and faded into the darkness. Longarm stood at the ragged edge of the pool of yellow light falling from the Exchange Hotel's entry, pulled his pistol, and carefully checked the loads. He slapped the loading gate closed, then slid the weapon back into the cross-draw holster high on his left hip. He pushed the hammer thong aside and made sure everything was as easy moving and slick as possible.

"No point puttin' this off," he said to himself.

The short walk to the Equity in the evil, biting cold wind took Longarm only a few seconds. He stopped in the shadows under the saloon's striped canvas awning and immediately noticed that the ever-present pack of mooching hounds had vacated their well-wallowed site around the front entrance. Leaning against the wall beside one of the saloon's curtain-poor front windows, he peered inside and leisurely scanned every nook and cranny.

Jack Hooper, his ruddy face covered with beads of sweat, stood behind the bar and appeared painfully uncomfortable. Swords, McCord, and Boggs slouched at the same back-of-the-room spot Longarm had used shortly after his arrival. Half empty whiskey bottles, scattered pasteboards, poker chips and cigarette butts littered the much abused green-felt tabletop. All three men looked well on their way to being drunker than a crew of fired cowhands. McCord's chin had dropped to his chest and his lips fluttered in silent snores. Swords and Boggs were locked in a heated argument that could be heard all the way into the street. Not one other soul occupied the normally busy saloon's main room.

As Longarm stepped through the door, he glanced at Hooper, who immediately took on the countenance of a man relieved of an unbearable burden. Longarm nodded at the bartender, strode across the room, and stopped a few feet from the only occupied table in the place. He'd picked a spot between the table and the door that would force Swords to turn around in his chair in order to see who'd entered the room and now stood menacingly behind him.

The plan worked. Longarm's spurs were still jingling when Boggs made an almost imperceptible motion at Swords with one finger and nodded. The south Texas gunman twisted in his run-down, cane-bottomed seat and glared over his shoulder. His upper lip curled back in a defiant sneer. "Well, I'll just be goddamned. Looka who's here, boys. I'll just kiss my own ass, if ain't the one and only Deputy U.S. Marshal Custis Long. Longarm of the law come to life."

Under the table, Swords kicked out at Mad Dog McCord and snapped the bleary-eyed gunman from his alcohol-induced nap. McCord jerked upright in his chair and, for several seconds, looked confused.

"I heard you wuz dead, lawdog," Swords said.

Longarm hooked his thumbs over his pistol belt. "Is that a fact? Well, as you can plainly see, you've been badly misinformed."

Swords's chair made a skin-crawler of a scraping

sound on the gritty, unfinished board floor as he pulled himself around to face the grim-visaged lawman. "Yeah," he grunted, then picked up a brimming shot glass, leaned back in his seat, and took a nibbling sip. He wiped his lips on the back of a dirty sleeve, then said, "Way I heard tell, the irate lover of a three-hundred-pound, bald-headed, snaggletoothed whore from down Las Cruces way kilt you for stealin' his rotten-crotched woman away from 'im. Heard he cut yer head off and stuck it on a pike for anyone passin' to get a gander."

Boggs, who sported the hangdog, deadpan look of a lost animal, rolled his one brown eye and one robin's-egg-blue eye almost into his skull and said, "Rumor goin' 'round has it you've always liked them gals what look like they mighta ate two or three of their sisters whole, Long." McCord and Swords laughed out loud. Slapped their knees at Boggs's feeble effort at belligerent, off-color humor.

Longarm didn't blink. "What are you and these other two certifiable idiots doin' in Tascosa, Swords?"

The tobacco-stained smile of self-satisfaction painted across the gunny's stubble-covered face vanished quicker than spit on a red-hot depot stove lid. "What's it to you, you badge-totin' bastard?"

As with a single voice, McCord and Boggs both perked up and drunkenly chimed in with, "Yeah, what's it to you, you badge-totin' sumbitch?"

Swords tipped his chair back on two legs. He fired a maduro panatela, blew a cloud of gunmetal-colored smoke in Longarm's direction, flipped his dying match to the floor, then growled, "You ain't got no paper on me, or my friends either, Long. We're as pure as newborn babes, as far as you federal boys is concerned. Just got into town a few hours ago. Ain't botherin' nobody. Ain't even moved from this here table. Don't believe me, ask that big ugly fucker behind the bar yonder."

Longarm locked eyes with the stone-cold killer and snapped, "I know you haven't caused any trouble yet, Swords. If you had, you'd of been picking parts of me out of your ass long before now. Just stopped by to make sure you knew that."

The sassy outlaw waved at Longarm with his lit cigar like he was shooing a pesky fly away. "So why don't you just get the fuck out of my face, Long. Head your ugly ass on back to wherever'n hell it is you done come from. That way, law-'biding citizens, like us boys, can finish our whiskey 'thout pukin' our individual guts up from the lawdog-who-just-fell-off-a-manure-wagon stench you're fuckin' givin' off."

Longarm pulled the tail of his suit jacket back and exposed the butt of the carved bone grips of his Frontier Model Colt pistol. "How 'bout if I come over there, snatch you outta that chair, and stomp a ditch in your arrogant ass. Then, when I'm finished, turn around, and stomp it drier'n August out on the Llano Estacado."

Swords tauntingly held up a pair of placating hands, as though horrified at the prospect. "Now, now, now, Marshal Long. No need for the federal law to go and get its dauber down. We're all well aware of just how tough a man you can be. We ain't lookin' for no fight. Are we boys?" He dropped the chair back down on all its legs and snarled, "Not just yet anyways."

"What the hell's that supposed to mean?" Longarm snapped.

Swords offered up a mocking grin. "Nothin', Marshal, didn't *mean* nothin' a 'tall. Not a damned thing. Now if you don't mind, my friends and I'd like to get back to the much needed relaxation and fellowship that drinkin', gamblin', and such provide after a long, hard ride. So do you think maybe you could just piss on outta here and leave us the hell alone?"

"Not until you can come up with an answer to my original question."

"Well, you're gonna be standin' there 'til after the Second Comin', and the imminent possibility of sulfurous hell a freezin' over, 'cause our business, whatever it might, or might not, be ain't none of yore 'n."

Boggs winked at McCord and in a whiskey-slurred voice said, "Yeah, lawman, our business, ain't none of yours, by God."

Longarm took another step toward the near-drunk trio. "In that case, you'd best pay strict attention to what I'm about to say—all three of you." He glanced from man to man and locked eyes with each for a few seconds before he bored in on Swords again. "I'm here on official business. Namely, as bodyguard for Judge Henry Cain. Should anything happen to the man while you stupid cocksuckers are in town—like him dying from an infected hangnail, or maybe falling down and breaking something important—I'll come find you boys. And trust me when I tell you, you won't like it when I do."

As though offended all to hell and gone, Selby Boggs wobbled to his feet. "Did I jus' hear you right? You a threatenin' us? Man's gotta have balls big enough to fill up a number-three grain scoop to be comin' right up in my face and threatenin' me whilst I'm havin' a quiet drink with my friends? God Almighty, but you must have some damned extra thick bark on your ass for such a move, mister."

McCord reached out, tugged at his friend's sleeve. "Sit back down, Boggs. Don't give this arrogant, law-pushin' son of a bitch a reason to kill you right here, right now. Come one, ole son, sit back down. We'll have another drink. Maybe go on over to Hogtown later. Git ourselves one of them Mexican whores what can pick up a nickel usin' her hands. Whaddya say?"

Boggs swayed like a creek-dwelling willow in a stiff breeze. He snatched the sleeve from his equally plastered friend's hand, and made a slow, stupid, and clumsy move for the big Smith & Wesson pistol awkwardly dangling between his legs.

In a blur of movement, Longarm took two more quick steps, whipped his Colt out, and brought the heavy barrel up across Boggs's face. Then, in one fluid shift of continuous momentum, he placed the open muzzle in Duncan Sword's ear and pushed the surprised man's head over onto his shoulder.

The five-and-a-half-inch piece of swinging steel had caught the drunker'n-hoedown-fiddler Boggs high on his right cheek and knocked him as cold as a frozen log-splitting wedge. The shocked gunny's hat flew off and landed on top of a nearby spittoon, glassy eyes flipped back into his head. He hit the seat of his chair like a dropped anvil, and landed in a sitting position. Then, his face plowed into the table, nose first, and landed hard smack in the middle of a puddle of blood and more than a handful of his broken teeth.

Covered with spattered gore, McCord pushed his chair away from the table. Hands in the air, he backed up against the wall and yelped, "For the love of Christ. You done gone and knocked all of poor ole Selby's damned teeth out. Hell, he didn't have many what was worth keepin' to start with. Shit fire. Broke his nose. Maybe all the bones in his cheek, too, looks like. Jesus, you didn't have to do that, you mean-assed son of a bitch."

With Longarm's pistol still pressed against his ear, Duncan Swords had his hands raised, looking like a carved, Italian-marble statue. Longarm leaned down in Swords's face almost nose to nose.

"Remember what I just said, and what you just saw, Swords. You and your boys best toe the line while you're in Tascosa—as long as I'm here. Otherwise, I'll throw all three of you in jail and forget about you. Now nod, like I've actually made myself as clear as a barrel of fresh rainwater." Swords's fingers twitched, but his head bobbed once.

Longarm backed all the way across the room to the Equity's front entrance before he holstered his weapon and stepped outside into a freshening wind blowing down Main Street from the west. He turned and almost immediately ran headlong into Rufus Tull. The old man, using a gnarled-up stick as a cane, had hobbled up undetected under the cover of darkness. He appeared to have aged twenty years since being shot.

Tull lashed out at Longarm with his newest leg and barked, "Watch where you're goin', you clumsy jackass. Swear if I warn't already hurt, you'd be pickin' yourself outta the dirt, by God."

Longarm stepped to one side. "Right sorry, Mr. Tull. Couldn't see you there. Mighty hard to spot anything smaller than a draft horse out here with no moon to light the way."

Tull made a sound like an angry wolf with its foot caught in a trap, flailed at the air with his cane, then continued limping his way toward the Equity's doorway. "Well, if you could get your head outta your lawdog ass long enough, maybe you woulda been able to see me, moon or not."

"Are you, by any chance, looking for Duncan Swords, Mr. Tull?" Longarm said, then pulled a cheroot from his vest pocket.

The elder Tull stopped with his hand on the Equity's front door. "What business is it of yours who I'm looking for, Marshal Long?"

"Oh, none. None at all, I suppose," he said while trying to light his smoke. He shook the match out and thumped it into the street. "Just wonderin' out loud. Thought you might be interested to know your friend Swords could well be a bit busy at the moment."

"Busy? What the hell 'er you talkin' about. Busy doin' what?"

Longarm picked a sprig of tobacco from his lip. "Last I took note, he was in the process of taking care of a case of the hardhead, and of doing a serious bit of nursing in the process, I think."

"Hardhead? Nursing? You're talkin' crazier'n a sunstruck lizard, Long. Have you been drinkin'? God Almighty, I ain't personally knowed a lawman yet what weren't a knee-walkin' drunk. Just goddamn typical's, all I can say."

"No. Nothing to drink for me tonight, Mr. Tull. Truth is, I simply haven't had the time to indulge."

Tull pushed the Equity's door open. Over his shoulder he called out, "Well, you can stop supposin'. Stop wonderin' about what I'm doin' and get the hell away from me. A man's business is his own, by God."

Longarm threw a knowing smile at Tull's hunched, disappearing back, chuckled to himself, then legged it for the jail and what he hoped would be a peaceful night of much-needed, uninterrupted, relaxing sleep.

Chapter 10

Longarm yawned himself awake the following morning to the smell of freshly brewed coffee. The nose-tingling aroma floated through every nook and cranny of the Oldham County Jail. His fuzzy tongue, which felt about the size of a saddle blanket, tasted like something akin to week-old wallpaper paste. The heavy, sweet bouquet from the stump juice almost deadened the smell coming from Bronson Tull's cell.

"Jesus, Tull. Why don't you use your chamber pot? Get rid of whatever crawled up your ass and died," Longarm called out. He rolled to a sitting position in the narrow, but oddly comfortable cot and noticed all his belongings from the hotel lay in a neatly arranged stack just outside the cell's open door.

First chance, he'd make certain sure Jesse Perkins got a nice tip for haulin' his stuff over. In another of the spartan cubicles directly across the open area between the shiny new steel-barred cubicles, Judge Cain slept as though dead behind privacy blankets draped over the bars, and snored like a hibernating grizzly bear.

Longarm attempted to stand. On the third try, he made

it to his feet, but came erect in an uncomfortable stoop for several seconds. One by one all the individual segments of his rigid, saddle-abused spine stubbornly snapped into place, like the links in a rusted logging chain. After another minute or so, punctuated by an abundance of farting and manly scratching, he silently stiff-legged his way past Cain's cot and into the outer office.

Nate Brice sat behind the sheriff's barely used mahogany desk, holding a cup of steaming, pungent-smelling Arbuckle's. He motioned toward the potbellied stove in the corner. "Fresh-brewed, Marshal Long. I make a mighty good pot a up-an-at-'em juice, even if I do say so my own self. But you should be warned, up front, it's strong enough to grow hair on a cavalry saddle. Sheriff Best calls it *potent*."

Without comment, Longarm stretched, nodded, then padded his slit-eyed way to the cast-iron stove. He poured a tin cup of the hot beverage, inhaled the fragrant perfume of Nate's effort, blew on the liquid for a second, then took the first, hesitant, careful sip. He nodded his approval, then ambled back across the room. Still half asleep, he pulled up a ladder-backed chair across the desk from Brice, slumped into it, then propped his socked feet in the only other empty seat.

After another wary swallow, Longarm coughed several times, before saying, "Mighty damned fine, Nate. Stick a spoon in this stuff and it'd stand up on its own. Just the way I take it. Cup or two should go a long way toward makin' me feel almost human again. You know, got to where, sometimes when I first wake up, feels like a three-hundred-pound stevedore stood over my bed and beat the hell out of me with a barrel stave. Can't imagine what gettin' out of bed's gonna be like in about twenty years. Probably have to be helped up by a nekkid woman."

Brice snickered at the image conjured up. "Well, I can certainly sympathize. I'm a lot younger than you, Marshal, and there's times when I feel the same way."

Of a sudden, Longarm's eyes popped fully open, and he cast a confused look at the deputy. "What're you doin' here this mornin' anyhow, Nate? Thought I told you to go home and stay there till you felt well enough to work."

Brice looked puzzled for about a second, then smiled. "Aw, hell, it's my job, Marshal. I'm supposed to be here. Sheriff Best wouldn't like it a damned bit if'n I didn't show up for work of a mornin'. You know that man's a former top hand from the LX spread, and he don't care a sack of horse fritters for slackers. No sir, not one little bit."

"Yeah, well that's all fine and dandy, but seems to me like I recall as how a dry-gulchin', skunk might have gone and hid in the dark last night and shot you. Do you, by chance, remember anything like that?"

"Oh, sure. You bet. 'Course I remember. But, you know, I'm feelin' fine this mornin'. Places them little ole bird pellets left ain't much worse than a nuisance case of prickly heat, right now. My wife, well, she went and slapped somethin' evil smellin' all over the whole damaged area. Girl said her grandmother called it bear grease—combination a hog lard, saltpeter, and some kinda store-bought ointment. Gotta admit the shit don't smell very good, but it sure 'nuff helped with the pain and itchin'."

Longarm placed his half empty cup on the desk, leaned back in the chair, and closed his eyes again. "Speakin' of jobs, Nate, Judge Cain wants me to deputize a couple of extra men. You, by any chance, know anyone who might be looking for a few days' worth of work? Dependin' on how the younger Tull's trial goes, maybe even a week's worth."

Brice straightened up and grinned from ear to ear. "Sure, Marshal. Winter's comin' on pretty quick, you know. All the big outfits in these parts like the LIT, Spade Diamond, Double H, LX, and LS done let lots of cowboys go till the spring roundup. That's why the hotel lobbies and saloons are full of 'em all the time. And over in Hogtown the mattress backs and gamblers are doin' a helluva business. So, to answer your question, I do know a coupla men who'd be perfect for the job. Absolutely perfect. Guarantee 'em, my very own self."

Longarm yawned, grabbed up his cup, and took another hit from the steaming liquid, then said, "Whoa momma, that's hot stuff. And who might these near-perfect fellers you know of be?"

"My brothers—Josh and Eli. Both done a bit of work for Sheriff Best in the past. And Josh was a real honest-to-God deputy marshal over in Mobeetie for almost a year. 'Bout as good as you'll find around these parts, Marshal. And maybe most important of all, they're honest. God Almighty, it's gettin' hard to find an honest man around Tascosa."

"Oh, I believe you, Nate. And I trust your judgment. Tell you what. Go ahead and get in touch with 'em. Have 'em come around to see me as soon as you can, and we'll talk it over. Make sure they understand I need their help right now, not two days, or a week from now."

Brice hopped up, grabbed his hat off the desk, slapped it on, and headed for the street. "Hey, I'll do 'em right this very minute. Pretty sure I seen 'em both a goin' into the North Star Restaurant for breakfast on my way to work this mornin'." He grabbed the knob, cracked the door a few inches, but stopped and turned back. "You went and got my bobbin wound up so tight here I almost forgot to tell you somethin' important. Have you seen the coach a sittin' down in front of the Exchange?"

"Coach? What coach?"

"Big ole, specially outfitted Concord. Grandest ride I think I've ever seen. Really somethin' exceptional. Busted a hub on one of the rear wheels, from the look of it, maybe even an axle. Probably gonna take two, maybe even three days to get 'er fixed."

Longarm glanced up from his cup and threw the boy a quizzical look. "So? What're you gettin' at, Nate? Busted Concord wheel hubs don't mean a thing to me."

Brice swelled up and hooked his thumbs over his pistol belt and looked right proud of himself. "Take a wild guess who owns that coach, or leastways who came to town in it." Longarm hesitated just long enough for the anxious deputy to add, "Go on, Marshal, try. Bet you'll never guess in a million years. Surprised hell out of me when I found out who it is."

"You're right, I probably won't be able to guess. Never was any good at such games. So come on and tell me, Nate. Who owns, or came to town in, the mysterious, special built Concord coach with a busted hub, parked down in front of the Exchange Hotel?"

Through a broad, toothy grin, Brice, said, "Ain't none other than Lila Crabtree, by God. Can you believe it? Tascosa's got the one and only, world-famous Lila Crabtree in our very own Exchange Hotel. Ain't that a whoopin' hoot?"

The name hit Longarm like a bolt of lightning straight out of the foggy past. The fleeting image of the lovely

Lila beckoning to him from a bed the size of a riverboat flashed across the backs of his eyes. He shook his head as though disbelieving. "Lila Crabtree? You're absolutely certain of that? Any possibility what you've heard is nothing more'n hopeful rumors, Nate?"

The still grinning deputy rocked back on his heels like a horse-trading rancher about to brag on his favorite bangtail. "Nope. Got it straight from Chauncy Pedigrew. Man was so excited I thought he just might piss his pants while he was tellin' me. Said the night clerk told him as how Miss Crabtree, and two or three of her personal toadies, dragged in about two o'clock this morning. Way I heard it, they were comin' from Dodge and headed for the opry house down in Amarillo when the coach hit a rock-bottomed pothole 'bout five miles out of town and the hub cracked."

"Did I hear you right?" Haystack-haired and sleepy-eyed, Henry Cain stumbled through the cell block door and headed for the coffeepot. He rubbed one eye with the back of his hand, then pawed around at his crotch as though digging for diamonds, as he poured himself a brimming cup. "Moment ago, thought sure I heard you say Lila Crabtree is in town. Wasn't dreaming was I?"

"No, sir, you ain't dreamin'. Heard me right." The smile of unfettered pride grew larger as it etched its way across Nate Brice's open, friendly face again. "The world-renowned Nekkid Lady her very own self. Right here in Tascosa. Just a few blocks from where we're a standin'. She's probably a layin' up in a rumpled bed down at the Exchange not wearin' enough to pad a crutch right this very minute. Can you imagine it? Jesus, I'd give a month's pay to see that."

Longarm said, "Bet if I closed one eye, stood on one

foot, and really concentrated, I could imagine just about damned near anything."

Brice shook his head. "You know, I been sittin' here all mornin', thinkin' 'bout her all rosy pink and nekkid as a jaybird, gents. God Almighty it's a hell of a thing, ain't it? Know I'm a married man and all, but, Jesus, we're talkin' Lila Crabtree here, maybe the best-lookin' female in the whole damned world. That is, if'n them pictures of her I seen on her posters is anywhere near accurate."

Cain said, "Sounds about right, you know. Woman's had graphically revealing posters plastered all over Amarillo for at least six months advertising her approaching visit. Town's entire male population, from age five to a hundred and five, has been lathered up for the past month about the prospect of her actually coming to town. Way I've heard it, she's supposed to present her *Wild Horse of the Stepps* show."

"*Wild Horse of the Stepps*, what's that?" Nate asked.

"Well, Deputy Brice, that's the very one wherein she reportedly rides onstage in the *altogether* while strapped to the side of a horse. Close friend of mine saw a performance in New York City. Said she might be doing little more than showing off her tits and ass, but the woman has some mighty fine tits and an absolutely spectacular ass. Said he'd be more than willing to bet you could bounce bullets from a .50-caliber Sharps off Lila Crabtree's ass."

"I saw her show in Virginia City several years ago." Longarm sounded bored when he said it, then stood and made his way to the washbasin. "Had me a close-up seat in the second row from the stage." As the other men watched and waited, he splashed water on his face and neck, and then dried himself.

"Well," Brice said.

"Well what?"

"Well, go on, for cryin' out loud," the inquisitive deputy moaned. "You're lookin' mighty pleased with yourself. You've got us on the hook now. So tell us. Did you actually get to see Lila Crabtree completely bare-assed, bare-breasted nekkid, totally exposed nooky and all, just like all them stories I've done heard?"

Longarm glanced from Brice to Cain and noted the look of joyful anticipation on both faces. "Wel-l-l-l," he drawled out as slowly as possible, "tell you boys what. Night I saw the infamous Miss Crabtree's act in Nevada City, if clothing had been gold dust the girl wouldn't have had enough on to fill a baby pissant's navel."

Brice threw his head back and yelped, "Yeeeee-hawwww. You reckon someone could get her to put on one of her shows while she's stuck here in Tascosa Marshal Long?"

"Well by God, that's all we need," Cain snorted. "Got enough of a circus with Bronson Tull's trial starting to-morrow morning. Then there's the threats against my life, ambushes in the street, explosions in my hotel room, and now a woman has arrived in town whose primary claim to fame is that she's brought brothel behavior out in public for display on the American stage. Next thing you know, troupes of demimondes from over in Hogtown will be performing acrobatic sex acts with circus clowns while leaning against the horses tied right outside McMasters's store down on Main Street."

"Well, guess that about covers just about everything I ever wanted to know about her," Brice said and pulled the door open.

"Wait," Longarm called, then turned to Cain. "What about it, Judge? I could use a hot meal. Why don't we

108

stroll on down to the North Star and have breakfast with Nate and his brothers. You can get a look at the boys I'm thinkin' 'bout takin' on as those extra deputies you've requested."

Cain didn't hesitate. "Sounds good to me, Marshal. Let's get dressed. We can speak with the proprietors while we're there. Make arrangements for some of our meals to be delivered to the jail until the trial ends. Yes, by God, sounds like a capital idea. But then, what about the possibility for ambush, Marshal?"

Longarm started back for his bunk. Over his shoulder he said, "Doubt we'll have a problem in broad daylight. Besides, we gotta eat. Don't we?"

Chapter 11

Near an hour later, a pleasant, plump, cherry-cheeked waitress bustled up and said, "You be sure'n call ole Ella if'n you need anything you can't find." She ushered Custis Long, Judge Cain, and Nate Brice to a table covered with a blue-checkered cloth located near the North Star Restaurant's only window overlooking Tascosa's Main Street. In pretty short order, they had steaming cups of black coffee sitting in front of them, along with a huge stack of homemade biscuits and a bowl of rib-sticking flour gravy dosed up with a combination of black and cayenne peppers.

Longarm had carefully eyeballed every nook and cranny of the busy feed lot before taking a seat, but saw nothing to raise any alarm bells. Sporting ten tables of various sizes and shapes, the single room's back wall had a large opening that looked directly into a cramped kitchen, where a lone Mexican cook bustled about in a flurry of concentrated activity over a massive cast-iron cookstove.

The mouthwatering scents of baking biscuits, flapjacks, frying bacon, sizzling eggs, and other such freshly

111

cooked wonders wafted through the busy restaurant and had the power to set a hungry cowboy's stomach to grumbling like a newly awakened grizzly, as soon as he entered.

Judge Cain's behind had barely hit his chair, when he sniffed at the menu selections listed on a battered chalkboard hanging over the cook's porthole. "Mighty rustic," he grumped. "Can't even begin to compare with any of Amarillo's better establishments. But I must admit most of those who frequent the place claim the cuisine, while bucolic in its origins, is quite good."

Longarm leaned back in his chair, took a puff from an already lit cheroot, then grinned. "Well, seems to me, you'd have to be a helluva poor cook to find a way to screw up *huevos revueltos y tortilla de huevos.*"

Deputy Brice soon spotted his kin and waved them over. Josh and Eli, while older than Nate, were, beyond any doubt, his brothers. All three men carried the same stringy-muscled, lanky build characteristic of hardworking cow men. Emerald-colored eyes and strong, angular jaws made their pleasant faces radiate confidence, when they smiled—and they did that often. All wore flat-brimmed hats, canvas vests, and leather-fringed shotgun chaps. They highlighted their ranch worker's attire with cross-draw holsters filled with Remington model 1875 revolvers. Longarm instantly recognized capable men as soon as he saw them.

The Brice brothers stood beside the table, their hats in their hands, and listened attentively as Longarm outlined his needs. Josh, who had a tinge of gray in his droopy mustache, glanced at Eli, and both nodded. "We'd be more'n happy to help out, Marshal Long. Hard time of the year right now. A man has to do whatever he can to get by. Old boys who've been around a spell claim we're in for another hard winter, so we'll take any work we can get. All you've got to do is point us in the right direction like a loaded six-shooter and pull the trigger. We'll do the rest."

Longarm turned to Henry Cain. "You have any objections, Judge?"

Cain stopped buttering a two-fisted biscuit long enough to wave a dismissive knife-filled hand. "You have my full faith and confidence, Marshal Long. I leave all such decisions to your very competent discretion, sir.

"Well," Longarm said, "since you boys've already had your meal, why don't you just stroll on down to the jail and wait for us there. We'll work out the details of how we're gonna do this dance later."

Josh Brice stuck out his hand. "Sounds good to us, Marshal. Me 'n Eli'll be waitin'."

Longarm stood, shook hands with both his new deputies, then resumed his seat and watched as they chinked their way to the door and disappeared. "Seem like mighty fine fellers, Nate."

Brice's ruddy cheeks flushed an even deeper red. "Thanks, Marshal Long. Sure they appreciate the vote of confidence you've shown by putting them to work. They're as good as you'll find 'round these parts."

With business out of the way, Longarm and his companions ordered up huge breakfasts. They'd managed to carve about halfway through a mountain of fried sausage and heaps of pancakes that dripped with fresh butter and thick blackstrap molasses when the North Star's front door popped open again.

Every inquisitive head in the place appeared to ratchet around at the same time, as a woman of remarkable beauty strode like a queen into the cramped room. The buzz of early-morning conversation and occasional laughter stopped, and, except for the clatter of movement from the kitchen, the entire room fell into a gasping silence. Men sat openmouthed, while their women slapped them on their arms or whispered from behind cupped hands.

Longarm glanced up from his plate. He swallowed a mouthful of half-chewed food, then wiped his lips on a napkin that matched the cloth covering the table. "Now that, gentlemen," he said under his breath, "is none other than the lady of our earlier interest, discussion, and speculation—the one and only, Miss Lila Crabtree."

Tall, willowy, and regal, the infamous Naked Lady wore her glistening auburn hair piled on a patrician head and covered with a hand-sized dove-gray, wedge-shaped hat. The hat matched a similarly colored short-waisted jacket and split riding skirt. An overlay of weblike white stitching in a faux Western motif accented the frilly collar of a blindingly white blouse tickling her chin. A dollar-sized cameo dangled from her neck on a gold chain. She carried a leather quirt decorated with a silver handle and slapped it against her thigh. Polished boots on child-sized feet sparkled from beneath her stylishly western skirt. With ease and grace, she strutted to the middle of the room, and glanced about. All the North Star's upturned, admiring faces followed her every movement.

Under his breath, and as much to himself as to anyone else, Longarm said, "Ain't it amazin', gents, how much power a beautiful woman can exert on people by just walkin' in a place and lettin' everyone get a good look at her?"

Within seconds Lila Crabtree's clear-eyed gaze swept

114

the room and fell directly on Longarm's smiling countenance. Full, sultry, ruby-colored lips parted, and all heads swiveled the beaming marshal's direction as the stunning beauty made a beeline for his table. "Why, Custis," she exclaimed, with her hand extended. Longarm stood and took her fingers in his. "Of all the towns, in all the places where we might have met, dear man, I never would have expected to accidentally stumble on you in an out-of-the-way place like Tascosa."

In the gallant and graceful tradition of all true Southern gentlemen cavaliers, Longram kissed the back of the famed actress's hand. "Most pleased to see you again, too, Lila. Most pleased. Been a long time, hasn't it, darlin'?"

She tilted her auburn head to one side, then leaned forward. He could feel her hot, sweet breath on his ear, when she whispered, "Much too long, my dear, Custis, much too long. I hope you still have fond memories of our time together in Nevada City. I know I do."

He spotted the cameo around her neck and carefully lifted it from her ample breast with one finger. "Astonishing likeness of you, Lila. Almost lifelike."

"Why, thank you, Custis. I had the piece made not long after we first met. It has always reminded me of you, dear man."

The judge and Deputy Brice sat rooted to their chairs—thunderstruck—until Longram turned and said, "Lila, I do believe it would make their day, possibly even their week, if you would please say hello to my companions, Judge Henry Cain and Deputy Sheriff Nate Brice. Both of these *gentlemen* have, this very morning, expressed great admiration for your amazing *talent* and striking beauty."

In turn, Lila Crabtree glanced at each man and gifted

him with an eye-fluttering, soul-stirring, coquettish smile and nod of her beautiful head. "Well, good morning, gentlemen. How kind of you to take note of my meager gifts. Please know I'm most flattered by such praise."

Both men stumbled to their feet and attempted chivalrous, but clumsy, bows. Much to Longarm's surprise and approval, Cain boldly blurted out, "As the room is near full, we'd be most honored if you'd sit at our table, Miss Crabtree. There's more than enough food for a dozen people. Do share our breakfast, we humbly insist."

Even Nate Brice, who sounded like an excited twelve-year-old, got into the act, when he offered his chair next to Longarm and stammered, "Yes, p-p-p-please seat yourself, Miss Crabtree. Take my ch-ch-chair, that way you'll find it much easier to talk with Marshal Long."

"Well, gentlemen," she said and swept into the proffered seat, "since my traveling companion and manager are both very ill and have taken to their beds, I gladly accept your kind offer, but only if you all promise to stop addressing me as Miss Crabtree. Sounds like an old-maid school teacher. Please, I beg you, do call me Lila."

For the next half hour, Longarm sipped at his coffee, dabbled with his food, and watched as the striking beauty easily and most skillfully captivated her tiny audience with witty and humorous tales of the numerous mishaps, missed connections, bad communications, and breakdowns she'd experienced on her most recent tour of the wild and wooly West.

She blithely spun wildly entertaining yarns amid the constant movement of those inquisitive souls bold enough to squeeze past the table and gape. Most of the gawkers made an awkward point of coming by just so they could bask in the reflected glory of perceived notoriety and uncommon beauty. Then they could hoof it down the street and brag to the first person they came upon about their great good fortune.

Longarm watched, listened, and puffed on a cheroot as he conjured up an image of those rewarded for their clumsy efforts with a fleeting glance of Lila Crabtree as they stood with thumbs hooked in their vest pockets, heads cocked back in triumph, and boasted to lesser beings, "Oh, my word, yes. Well, I've just this moment come from the North Star, where I personally met, and even spoke with, the notorious Naked Lady of New York, Paris, and London stage fame. Beautiful woman. Beautiful woman. Yes, I must say. But one of highly questionable virtue, if you ask me."

He came out of his reverie in time to hear Lila say, "My unplanned appearance here in Tascosa is just so typical of the maladies that constantly befall me, gentlemen. Why, Mary Boucher, my traveling companion, fell violently ill the very night we left Dodge."

"How dreadful," Judge Cain said.

"Terrible thang to have happen on the trail," Nate Brice added.

"Let me tell you," Lila went on, "it is a difficult handful to manage when your six-foot-nine black chaperone is hanging out the window of an energetically bouncing Concord coach, heaving up everything she's eaten from the previous two weeks. And then, a few hours into that ghastly ordeal, John Trotter, who manages my business affairs and arranges these jaunts, came down with the same malady, whatever it is."

"Oh, you poor, poor dear."

"Why that's just awful."

"And then, lo and behold, the next thing I knew, we'd

117

barely passed into the wildness of the Indian countries when some of the savages attacked our coach. The driver swears they were renegade Kiowas, but I must admit those poor people were a scraggly looking lot and nowhere near a match for our brand of firepower. Then, on top of everything else wayward that has transpired, yesterday we dropped into a pothole so deep it did something I'm told might well be irreparable to one of the wheels."

"Musta been one tremendous big hole to bust a hub," Brice mused.

"As God as my witness, gentlemen," Lila went on, "I got down from my coach and gazed into that chasm and saw the flames of perdition. A short time later, my driver suggested we stop over here in Tascosa until repairs could be made, and my escorts could recuperate to the point of being able to travel again."

Longarm arched an eyebrow. "How long do you expect to be in town, Lila?"

She shot him a quick, fetching glance, winked, and said, "Well, it appears we might be in town for several days, my dear Custis."

"Really?"

"Oh, yes. Early this morning, after nearly an hour of heated discussion, my driver assured me something on the coach was so badly damaged that I've been compelled to pay a local wheelwright an exorbitant amount to ride all the way into Amarillo. He claims an inability to fabricate a vital part on site and must make the trip to purchase it. The entire situation is most distressing, but unavoidable, I suppose. Not sure I believe it, but that's what he said."

Longarm's eyebrow went up even higher. "Well, then,

perhaps we can take a ride this afternoon, or tomorrow. A jaunt into the countryside and a picnic lunch just might be the remedy that momentarily relieves your mind from all the unpleasantness you've experienced thus far. Do you good to get away from your sick companions and the frustration of dealing with the damage to your coach."

Unseen sparks flew between them as she smiled and reached over to take his hand in hers. "Custis, you sly devil. That's such a wonderful idea. Here I'd thought sure my days would be nothing more than boring times spent in my room. You've always known exactly what I need to make me feel better, haven't you? And, of course, there was an unknown reason for me picking this particular outfit to wear today."

"I always try to please a lady, Lila. You know that. And I love your riding outfit."

A demure smile preceded her saying, "Well, gentlemen, I thank you for your hospitality, but I believe the time has come for me to get back to the hotel and check on my suffering associates." As she rose, her hand slid off Longarm's, dropped unseen between his legs, and deftly gave his cock and balls a quick squeeze. Difficult as it was, he managed to maintain control when she smoothed her riding skirt and added, "Do be sure and call on me at your earliest convenience, Custis. A spirited ride, after the past few days of nothing but one catastrophe after another, would surely do me wonders. I'll be waiting for you and thinking of our time in Nevada City."

All three men stood for the famous actress's departure. Cain did a slight, but gracious, bow. "Our sincere thanks for a most pleasant visit, Miss Lila. Sure I speak for each of us, and every man in town, when I say that we genuinely hope to see you again."

Lila gave her head a coquettish tilt. "Well, Judge, if not here in Tascosa perhaps I'll see you in Amarillo, when I do my next performance. I'm almost certain you'll enjoy it. Good day, gentlemen. Don't forget, Custis."

Time appeared to stand still, once more, as she imperially strutted past the gaping occupants and tittering buzz that commenced from each table and continued past the North Star's front entrance. Longarm watched her cross Main, stop in the street long enough to talk with another bold admirer, and then proceed on to the hotel. A knowing smile creased his tanned and weathered face. Appeared as how Rosarita and Consuelo might not enjoy his company after all. When satisfied Lila had made the short journey safely, he turned and started to resume his seat.

Cain held up a hand and said, "Bronson Tull's trial starts tomorrow morning at ten o'clock, Marshal. I'd like to make certain of any plans you have for my safety with our new deputies. In that spirit, I think it best we head back to the jail and review all preparations and strategies pursuant to that effort."

Longarm nodded and shoved his hat back on. "Sounds good to me, Judge. Let's go get 'er done. We'll swear these fellers in, then discuss how we're gonna keep you safe."

Chapter 12

Longarm leaned over Sheriff Jim Best's desk and pointed out the various areas he'd outlined on a rough map of Tascosa's courthouse, jail facilities, along with the streets and alleys surrounding the entire area. All the Brice brothers appeared totally concentrated on what he said. Judge Cain detached himself from the group, stood to one side, rubbed his chin, and listened as the plans for his continuing protection unfolded.

"At least two of us must be with Judge Cain on the daily walk from here to the courthouse every morning, and stay with him at all times during the duration of the trial," Longarm said. "While it is, admittedly, a very short stroll—barely more than a hundred feet from the jail's front entrance to the courthouse door—we've already been made painfully aware of just how dangerous that brief jaunt could turn out.

Nate rapped the desk with his knuckles. "I'll be the first deacon to shout an enthusiastic amen to that one, Marshal. Wounds to my side are still a nuisance, in spite of my wife's efforts. Beginning to believe the effectiveness of this stinkin' stuff she used on me this mornin' has done gone and wore off."

Longarm pulled a cheroot from his vest pocket and jabbed it into his mouth. "Look, boys, what I'm sayin', in no uncertain terms, is that every one of us has gotta be on his toes at all times."

Eli tilted his head to one side, then slapped the weapon on his hip. "Pistols, rifles, shotguns, knives, ax handles. How do you want us equipped out, Marshal Long?"

"Good question, Eli. For the most part, I'd like everyone to carry short-barreled shotguns loaded with heavy-gauge buckshot, in addition to your preferred side arm. Don't want any of you to take any unnecessary chances, boys. Have not one doubt you're all great with a pistol, but a shotgun really goes a long way to getting even the most aggressive mankiller's full and undivided attention. Ten-gauge popper works in just about any worrisome situation I've ever seen. Those big blasters really can separate the men from the boys, and damned fast."

Longarm stopped, waited for possible comment, then continued. "Additionally, if the judge has to go outside the jail or courthouse for any other reason whatever while the trial is in recess—such as a walk downtown for lunch, or a trip to the outhouse—the same plan applies. We've got to make every effort to keep any of his moving around beyond the confines of these walls to daylight hours, and limit all other movement, where possible as well."

Nate rubbed his arm, flicked a glance at Longarm, then said, "Are we truly faced with that dangerous a situation, Marshal? Mean, hell, I was there when the ambush

122

happened, but this all sounds like any one of us could be murdered at the drop of a hat."

"Given the venom contained in the written threats he's already received thus far, along with the two recent attempts on his life, we mustn't let our guard down for one second, until such time as Judge Caine is safely back in Amarillo."

Josh Brice picked a thin splinter of chewed wood from between his teeth. He held it like a pointer and drew an imaginary circle around the scribbled courthouse and jail on Longarm's makeshift map. "Can I suggest, Marshal, that it might be a good idea for some of us to search this entire area every morning, before making that hundred-foot walk across the street. An open search, an obvious show of determined force, may not work out as the be-all and end-all to stop another shootin', but I'd bet seein' us prowlin' around will, at the very least, give our mysterious rival, or rivals, something new and serious to think about."

Longarm flashed a big grin at his newly sworn deputy and slapped the man on the shoulder. "Damn good idea, Josh. As a man much wiser than me once said, 'All of us are a lot smarter than any one of us.' So whatever you boys can come up with that has the possibility of putting our potential assassin off balance, just speak right up. Don't be shy. I've never claimed perfection, and have no problem using other people's proposals in a situation as deadly as this one now appears. So, do you have other thoughts or suggestions?"

For several seconds the brothers glanced back and forth at one another. Eventually, all three shrugged their inability to come up with more in the way of helpful ideas. Finally, Longarm poked at the map with his finger and said, "Then that's the way we'll handle the situation, until such time as events might deem otherwise. For today, I'd like the three of you to stay close to Judge Cain here at the jail. You're not to leave him alone except when he's back in the cell block. I'll walk the streets, check on the town, and take care of any problems that might come from the outside. Tomorrow we'll put the details of what was just discussed into action. Is everyone on board? Everyone understand? Any problems at all with what's been said?"

Nate made a tentative motion with one hand. "Just one final question, Marshal. Why don't you let me take care of things out in the street? I'm more familiar with the town, and its citizens, and there's really no need for you to have to do it."

"Well, I appreciate your kind offer, Nate," Longarm said, "but our ambusher wants the judge dead, and he knows, by now, that you've been hurt. That might not sound like much of a disadvantage, but trust me, you need to be on top of your game for whoever is out there lying in wait. Given that I'm the most experienced man here, think it should fall to me to make sure the streets stay calm and safe. Does that make sense to you?"

Without hesitation, Brice nodded. "Yessir. Makes perfect sense."

Longarm turned to Henry Cain. "You have anything to offer, or any further questions you'd like answered, Judge? Need to speak up if you do."

Cain came to attention. "Your preparations are well thought out and sound most satisfactory to me, Marshal Long. Of course, the unexpected is always a possibility, but we'll just have to take care of those events as they transpire. I'm completely comfortable with the arrangements as you've outlined them, and feel my safety is assured with such a fine cadre of men guarding me."

"Good," Longarm said. "In that case, I'm off to make my first turn around town. Think I'll head south to Main, then west to the footbridge over the creek, and back along the south side of main to McMasters, thence back to the jail. Should you hear shots, or if you are informed by witnesses that events have gone amiss, one or two of you can come a running to check on me, boys. When I'm walking that route, no matter what happens, at least one of you must stay here with Judge Cain. Everyone on board?" Nodding heads brought the meeting to a close.

A rust-colored sun bored through ragged cloud cover and the swirling dust was carried by a chilling blow from out of the west. Longarm hunched against the wind and made his way down McMasters Street, past Shelton's drugstore, and on to Main. He'd walked the same route at least three times since his arrival in town and now felt a comfortable familiarity with the stores, residences, rail fences, trees, water troughs, hitching posts, and numerous outbuildings all along the route back to the Exchange Hotel. A number of people passed on the street, but nothing appeared out of the ordinary.

He'd just stepped into Spring Street, sometimes referred to as the Dodge City Trail by locals—because that very spot began or ended, depending on your viewpoint, the meandering route north to Kansas from Tascosa—when he heard a dog yelp in pain a number of times. Veering into the middle of Main near the Exchange Hotel's southeast corner, his gaze fell on the front entrance of the Equity Saloon. The affable pack of lazy hounds that made their home virtually in the establishment's front door were scattering in different frenzied directions.

Duncan Swords and Selby Boggs leaned against the wall near the cantina's entrance and watched their whiskey-bottle-carrying friend Marion Mad Dog McCord kick the bejabberous hell out of the biggest, friendliest, red-bone hound in the easygoing pack. A deep, profound, and overwhelming sense of anger, with any man who would mistreat a harmless animal in such a way, swept over Longarm in a wave of seething resentment and red-eyed anger. Any man who'd commit such an act of cruelty would likely do the same to people, without any compunction whatever. Blood rose up Longarm's neck and colored already cold ears.

McCord had his back turned, consumed with his brutal dance. Longarm materialized out of a swirling dust devil like a vengeful ghost, bone-gripped pistol in hand. Swords and the previously chastised Boggs, eyes blackened, sporting a split, scab-covered nose, swollen to the size of a sod-buster potato, made motions as though they planned to warn their friend. Longarm waved them into twitching silence. Without so much as saying a word, he'd made it abundantly clear they would pay a heavy price for any interference.

Longarm got to within arm's length of the drunken animal abuser, before he growled, "That's enough, you stupid son of a bitch. Kick that poor beast one more time and I'll put a bullet in your dumb ass quicker'n double-geared lightning."

McCord twirled around so fast he came nigh to falling

down. Too late, the sodden widow maker and dog stomper realized his gun hand was occupied with a half-filled bottle of scamper juice strong enough to raise blood blisters on a boot heel. Red-eyed, and seething with whiskey-induced courage, he yelped, "Gaw-damn. You almos' made me pissh myseff. Gotta lotta nerve comin' up 'hine a man yellin' on 'im lak 'at. Yew cocksuckin' do-rights thank yew kin jesh by Gawd do as yew pleash, doan chu?"

McCord smeared his filthy sleeve across slobber-covered lips, lifted the amber-colored quart jug, and sucked down another gulping slug. He swayed like a flag-pole in a stiff wind. Finger-sized streams of tongue-scorching liquor flowed from both sides of his mouth down a grimy neck and into the collar of his ratty, bib-front shirt.

Longarm gritted his teeth, then whacked the bottle with the barrel of his pistol. A shower of splintered glass and whiskey rained down on McCord's filth-encrusted face and upper body. The angry drunk stumbled backward two full steps, regained his balance, then hurled the intact neck of the shattered jug into the street. "Thash hit, by Gawd. I gonna kill tha hell outta yewer soory ash. Gwin a do'er rat now. Seein's as how it's wha' I done comed all the way down here to the back side a hell fer in firsh place, killin' yer law-pushin' ass should be easy 'ern eatin' Mom's hot apple pie."

McCord staggered from foot to foot, as his right hand fumbled for the grip of his pistol. Longarm shook his head in disbelief at the stupidity of the move. His first thunderous shot blew a hole in the top of the inebriated gunny's right foot and, because of their close proximity to each other, the massive slug knocked the man's leg from under him. He yelped like the dog he'd just been kicking and went down like a freshly felled tree, landing in the street on his face so hard that this head bounced off the hard-packed dirt like a kid's rubber ball. He twitched for about another five seconds, then fell into unconsciousness.

From the corner of his eye, Longarm spotted Selby Boggs, just as the man made an incredibly poor decision on how to respond to the situation. Boggs pulled his pistol out, almost had it up to fire, when a second booming blast delivered a red-hot 255-grain bullet that punched a thumb-sized hole between Boggs's ribs a few inches left of his breastbone. The massive chunk of lead shattered his black heart on its way to an exit that sprayed a gob of blood, bone, and gore the size of a washtub onto the wall behind him. Stiff-legged and glassy-eyed, with a look of total surprise stamped on his face, Boggs staggered into the street, fired harmless shots into the dirt, and then fell to the ground graveyard dead within a few feet of the already unconscious McCord.

Before Duncan Swords had time to spit, Longarm was on top of him. Quicker'n a bull can get to a hole in a fence, the surprised gunman had Longarm's Frontier model Colt's five-and-a-half-inch barrel pressed almost three inches into his aching gut.

"Didn't have no part in it, Long," he squealed. "Ain't got nothin' against dogs. Haven't touched my weapon. You can surely see it like it is. Swear I didn't even move. Jesus, cain't you pull back a bit. Damned gun barrel's pushin' on my liver. Hurts like hell."

With their hat brims touching, Longarm snarled, "I'm only gonna say this once, Swords. Want you out of town as fast as you can get on a horse and go. Pick up those other gobs of shit behind me on your way out and take 'em with you. Don't come back as long as I'm here. Is there any part of what I just said that you didn't understand?"

Beads of sweat the size of a man's thumb ran down Swords's forehead and formed tiny rivers moving toward his nose. "Oh, you were as clear as a bucket of fresh rainwater, Marshal. I'll have 'em both up and outta here quick as I possibly can. Guarantee you won't be a seein' Duncan Swords around these parts anytime in the foreseeable future."

Knots of murmuring townfolk had gathered in the street behind them. Longarm pulled his pistol barrel out of Swords's gut and took a step back into the street. Armed with shotguns, Josh and Eli Brice thundered up and began dispersing the crowd. "Get the hell away. Ain't nothin' here for you loafers to see. This is official business, so get on back to yours," Josh shouted.

Eli darted over to a protective spot beside Longarm and waved his big popper at the still gathering crowd. He leaned toward Longarm and under his breath said, "What the hell's goin' on here, Marshal? What happened? Are you okay?"

Longarm made an all encompassing wave at the three gunmen with his own weapon. "These boys are leavin' town, Eli—right by God now, as a matter of pure fact. Do me a favor and see all of 'em across Tascosa Creek, once Swords has collected their possibles and such."

Josh Brice arose from having examined Selby Boggs, pointed at the corpse with his shotgun, then said, "This 'un here appears pretty much dead, Marshal Long. Want him out of town, too?"

"Damned right. Him, the one with the hole in his foot, and that sneering, arrogant son of a bitch standin' over there by the wall. See to it, boys. Then make sure all these people get off the street. Nothing else here for 'em. This gunpowder dance is over."

"Sure you're okay, Marshal?" Eli said.

Longarm holstered his still smoking weapon, then stomped away from the new deputy without replying. Like a man on a mission, he headed for an ancient live oak a few doors down from the Equity Saloon's entrance. The Brice brothers watched as Longarm squatted over a dog stretched out on the ground next to the tree.

He scooped the injured animal up and carried the beast to its favorite hollowed-out spot on the ground near the Equity's front door. He carefully laid the dog in the shallow depression, then patted it on the head. The pitiful creature licked Longarm's hand, so he patted him again. Sad-eyed and hurting, the dog flicked its tail against the dirt and groaned, as Longram stood and removed his hat.

Eli Brice stepped to Longarm's side. "He don't look real good, Marshal."

"No, he don't, Eli. But it's been my experience that dogs do have remarkable powers of recuperation," Longarm said, then stuffed his hat back on. "Be willing to bet, it'll take that hole I put in McCord's foot a hell of a lot longer to recover than it does for this ole boy to get back up on his feet. Had a big ole pooch that looked almost like this one when I was a kid. He darted out in the road chasin' a chicken and a wagon ran over him. Thought sure he would die. But he didn't. 'Bout a week later he was up and doin' fine. Maybe three years passed and then one day he must have tried to outrun a westbound train that passed near our place. Cut his hind leg off. 'Course it took 'im a bit longer, but he recovered. Got around damn near as well on three legs as four. Damned dog lived almost ten years."

"Amazin'."

"Yep. And you know, seems like the younger they are, the quicker they mend. This poor old skillet licker might be damaged beyond redemption. But just in case there's a chance, do me a favor, son. Get a piece of blanket and cover him."

The deputy laid his shotgun across his arm as his brother strode up. "Was the dustup over nothin' more'n a dog, Marshal?"

Longarm snapped a pointed glance at the boy. "Not entirely. The unfortunate events that just transpired here would've happened, sooner or later, given the kind of men involved. McCord just threw some kerosene on the fire a bit sooner than Swords anticipated, or wanted. All three of 'em probably expected the fight to come later, and over something a lot more deadly that would've involved one or more of us ending up facedown in the dirt when it was over."

"Oh, I'm not questionin' what you did, Marshal. Just wanted to get clear on how it all came to pass."

"Good. Well, it's over now anyway. Everything's under control, so let's get back to the plan."

As the brothers started away, Josh turned back and said, "Oh, think you might want to know. Few minutes after you left the jail, Tull's lawyer showed up. Feller from Amarillo folks call Racehorse Alvin Parker. 'Sposed to be hell on wheels when it comes to savin' bad men from the gallows, Marshal."

Longarm's gaze flew past the brothers to the Exchange Hotel's entrance. Lila Crabtree burst from a knot of gawkers outside the door and headed in his direction in a dead run. She threw herself into his arms, clung to his neck, and sobbed as though they'd been long-lost lovers who'd been parted for years.

He glanced over Lila's shoulder at the deputies and said, "Since Judge Cain is there, I don't think we'll have to worry any about Racehorse Parker. You boys go on back to the jail. I've got something else to take care of down here right now. Tell Nate I'll be back in an hour or so."

Longarm gently peeled Lila off his neck, stepped back and tipped his hat. "You've always had the ability to surprise me, Lila."

She wiped a huge tear from the corner of one eye, then toyed with a button on his vest. "You've been playing rough with some really bad boys haven't you, Custis?"

"You could say that, darlin'."

She looped her arm into his and guided him toward the hotel's open door. "I heard men in the hotel lobby saying you'd been killed. Please forgive me for overreacting the way I did, but I was overjoyed to see that you'd come to no harm. Think we should retire to my room for a few minutes." She twisted a finger inside his shirt and drew circles on his naked chest. "That way, I can thoroughly check you out to make sure there are no hidden wounds on you—*anywhere*. We can see if it's possible for me to help you unwind after such a wearisome and deadly morning's work. I'm certain it's terribly difficult for any man to have to shoot two people in the street so early in the day."

"Are we thinkin' about the same kind of *relaxation*, Lila?"

"Absolutely, my dear Custis. It's the brand of relaxation I haven't experienced since our last bout of *relaxing* in Nevada City."

"Ah. Sounds like exactly what I need more'n anything else right at the moment. An hour's worth of pure, unadulterated *rest and repose*."

Chapter 13

Longarm tossed his gun belt onto the only chair in Lila Crabtree's spartan hotel room. "I've come to believe all the accommodations in this place are the same. Your room looks exactly like the one I had down the hall for a few hours right after I arrived. Bed, table, one chair, dresser, washstand, small coal-fired stove, even the same picture on the wall. And damned if this don't look like an exact duplicate of the frayed rug on the floor—even down to the dirty footprints."

Lila stood before a badly silvered mirror cracked across one corner. Head bent, she worked at the clasp on the gold chain around her neck. "I've slept in worse places, Custis."

He slipped off his string tie, vest, and shirt, then draped them over the back of the chair. Moved in behind Lila. Placed his hands on her hips, then ran them up to her ample bosom. Tenderly cupping her breasts, he rolled each nipple between his fingers and thumbs. At the same time, he bent down and nibbled on the side of her neck.

The heady scents of expensive French perfume and the taunt, almost glowing, flesh of a passionate woman filled his nostrils. "Don't think I ever mentioned anything about it being a terrible place, Lila, only that all the rooms look the same." He sent hot breath into her ear, then went back to biting her on the neck. "Hell, it could be a stable in El Paso, and I'd still want you right there on the floor—in the straw."

She groaned, dropped the cameo necklace onto the dressing stand with one hand, reached between their arching bodies with the other and squeezed his already rigid rapier of love. "God but I've missed this *thing* of yours. Had an unfulfilled craving for every inch since our time in Nevada City." She eased her head back against his chest, turned slightly and whimpered into his ear. Her grip on his superheated prong tightened. Too soon, she pulled her hand away, but rewarded him by aggressively rubbing her hips against the massive and still growing bulge in his pants.

Growing more excited by the second, Longarm ran one hand down Lila's board-flat stomach to the split front of her riding skirt, palmed the steamy mound between her legs and began a slow massage. He heard a sharply abbreviated breath hitch in her throat, and an agonized groan of lusty hunger oozed from her lips.

Smiling to himself, he said, "Why, Lila. You're not wearing anything in the way of undergarments, are you darlin'? When on earth did you get so bold? The girl I remember, from years ago back in Nevada City, would never have dared to appear in public with nothing more than the flimsy fabric of a blouse and skirt between her womanly treasures and the rest of the world."

Lila gasped, leaned back against him, clutched at the unrelenting hand still caressing her breast, then grabbed at his crotch again. In a voice that dripped with pent-up,.

volcanic lust, she hissed, "The girl you met in Nevada City grew up and became a full-fledged woman, Custis. Happened right after my mother stopped traveling around the world with me. All woman now, Custis. And, as you, above all other men should know, women do have needs. Right now I need one of your very special *treatments*, Doctor Long. The unique one that involves that beautiful, heat-hardened shaft you're rubbing against my inflamed cheeks right now."

She twirled around inside his embrace, tilted her head to one side, and waited for their mutually approaching lips to lock. He ran his hands up under her arms, lifted the shameless girl even higher, as he leaned forward to meet full, pouting, parted lips with his. Their mouths came together with a violence Longarm hadn't really expected. For a moment he thought she might suck the fillings right out of his teeth.

She threw her arms around his neck, forced his lips apart with her own broad, snakelike tongue, and filled his eager mouth. Fond memories of that incredible tongue flooded his consciousness. Beyond doubt, Lila Crabtree possessed the longest and widest he'd ever encountered. Longarm responded to her sensual use of the nearly inhuman appendage exactly the way she had most likely expected he would. His arms slipped around her tiny waist and tightened. He lifted her completely off the floor and drew her to him.

The passion-besotted girl's knees came up. She scissored the powerful legs of a dancer around his waist, then rubbed her steaming, hot sex against his bulging cock in a scalding, circle-eight motion clearly designed to drive him straight to distraction.

Longarm dropped one hand to her muscular behind

and pulled her even tighter against him. His other hand came up between their writhing bodies and pawed at her breasts until he'd opened her blouse and could get his lips around a heat-hardened, almost diamondlike, blood-engorged nipple. He worried the stiff tip of her breast with a wet, insistent tongue, then licked his way back up to her open mouth.

Stumbling steps moved them to the bed's edge. He leaned forward, but she refused to relax her viselike grip around his waist. With some effort, he broke his mouth away from her tonsil-tickling tongue long enough to say, "You've gotta let go of me, darlin'. Cain't get much done while I'm still wearin' these pants."

Lila dropped to the bed in a sitting position and immediately tore away at what little still covered her ripe, flushed body. In no time at all, she lay wantonly sprawled before him completely naked, legs spread to the maximum, expectant, arms extended. "Come on, Custis, don't keep me waiting any longer, darlin'. Feels like I'm gonna explode right here, right now. And when I do, I want you inside me. I've fantasized about a repeat performance like this for years. Sure you can live up to it?"

He teasingly exhibited no urgency, as he slowly stripped off his pants and cotton balbriggans. All the while her fevered eyes locked on to his rampant prong. With growing urgency, she diddled herself into a frothy frenzy. Not satisfied with his erotic display, Lila rolled onto her knees, grabbed his blood-engorged dingus and sucked it so far into her mouth that the sensitive tip rested against her tonsils. Her efforts to pull the raging beast in all the way proved futile, but well worth the effort.

Longarm gently slid calloused fingers into the lust-addled girl's hair, rocked back on his heels beside the bed and let her have her way. Near as he could remember, Lila Crabtree's surprising new talents far exceeded anything he could recall from their distant past.

After almost ten minutes of the most intense sexual pleasure he could reasonably endure, she flipped onto her back again. "Now, Custis. Stick that beautiful thing in me, right now." As he took his time crawling up between Lila's legs, her hand found his steely, saberlike erection again, and guided his first powerful thrust into her moist, waiting body.

A minute or so into their initial delirious humping, she grabbed his hips, arched her back, and banged her pubis against him as hard as she could. Then she rubbed her open sex back and forth across his crotch, then moaned like a female mountain lion.

At one point, she ran both hands down between them, placed her fingers inside the lips of her pussy and pulled it open as wide as she could, exposing every moist, slick, reddened inch to their hectic, grinding efforts. Such blatant displays of unbridled carnality spurred him to even greater effort, and sharpened his fiery performance.

They fell into an extended, ecstatic rhythm of thrusts, parries, then retreats, reposts, feints, loving attacks, and sweaty, noisy, gushing counterattacks. After nearly an hour of such action, their hectic lovemaking drew to its logical, exhausted conclusion.

Covered in sweat that dripped onto Lila's heaving breasts, Longarm felt her swelling around the shaft of his cock. Her breathing came in rapid, hard pants. Spasmodic waves of fleshy tremors rolled through her bucking body, as her upward momentum intensified.

Of a sudden, she threw both arms around his neck, pulled him down and thrust her tongue into his mouth, then licked her way to the hollow of his throat. "Harder, Custis.

139

Harder, darlin'," she demanded, then grabbed his ass with both hands and socked herself against him as though she expected to be welded there in liquid rapture forever. Her orgasm pumped him bone dry.

For some minutes after he'd finished and embraced her as though tomorrow would never see sunshine, the lovely Lila's sweat-drenched, lava-hot depths closed around him and continued with a seemingly endless series of quivering, spasmodic convulsions.

Once the intensity of their lovemaking had ebbed, and he'd begun to grow flaccid inside her superheated body, Longarm tried to separate himself from her embrace. She clung to his neck and, as though drugged, whispered, "Not yet, dear Custis. Please stay inside me a bit longer. Just a bit longer, don't pull out yet, I beg you."

Tenderly, he kissed her forehead, the tip of her nose, her lips. "Close your eyes, Lila. Promise you I won't go until you're fast asleep. Part of the entire and complete Doctor Custis's full body *treatment*, darlin'. How's that?"

"Yes. Until I'm a . . . s . . . leep. Trea . . . ment," she mumbled, and within seconds had tumbled headlong into a deep and contented slumber.

He wasn't exactly sure how long he stayed there with her, but some time later Longarm reluctantly untangled himself from her satiated embrace. Before attempting to get dressed, he stood naked beside the bed—in admiring silence—for a moment, just to make sure he hadn't thoughtlessly disturbed her.

"My God, but you are one helluva beautiful woman, Lila," he whispered, then pulled a rumpled sheet, soaked with the heavy scent of their torrid bout, over her still-glowing body. He gave himself a quick, but thorough, rinse in the washbasin, redressed, kissed her one more time, then quietly slipped out.

As the early-afternoon sun attempted to chew its way through angry, low-hanging, gray-black clouds, Longarm hit the Exchange Hotel's front door, shoved a cheroot into his mouth, and heeled it for the jail. At the corner of McMasters and Main, he spotted a churning knot of people that milled around the entrance of the county's brand-new stone building. While a relatively small group, they appeared, to him, a bit on edge. As he trudged in their direction, several spotted his approach, pointed on the sly, then conferred with their fellows behind cupped hands.

The crowd parted as the wary lawman stepped onto the jail's abbreviated board porch. He nodded and touched the brim of his hat to those bold enough to meet his gaze, but noticed no one bothered to speak.

The door popped open. As Longarm reached for the knob. Nate Brice appeared in the open entryway and seemed surprised by his arrival. Brice's eyes lit up. "Marshal, boy, am I glad to see you," he said, then grabbed Longarm by the elbow, pulled him inside, and slammed the door shut.

Chapter 14

Longarm cast a quick, nervous glance around Sheriff Best's crowded outer office. "What the hell's goin' on, Nate? Who let all these people in? There ain't no way in hell to protect Judge Cain with so many folks all crowded up inside our office like this. Shit, anyone of 'em could shoot 'im 'fore we could stop 'em."

Brice nodded his tense agreement, then leaned close, as though he had a secret that needed revealing. "Thank God you're back. And, trust me, I know, Marshal. I knew exactly how you'd feel about all this soon's you found out. But you weren't around when this bunch showed up, and they just fogged in on us so quick we couldn't stop 'em. Couldn't shoot 'em. Most of these men've been friends of ours since we was kids."

Longarm threw his head back in disgust. "Jesus, save me from the perils of friendship. Well, get on with it. Tell me about the problem at hand."

"Believe me, Marshal Long, my brothers and I know exactly how you feel. Look, 'pears to me an' Josh an' Eli as how we mighta done got us something of a political predicament a goin' here. Maybe you can settle these folks' minds a bit. Near as I've been able to tell, they're a delegation of some of the town's more prominent and concerned businessmen. Judge Cain ain't been a havin' much luck with 'em. Seems they're a mite upset 'bout the shootin's this afternoon, and all."

"Well, now is that a fact?"

"Yessir, it is at that."

"Correct me if I'm wrong, Nate, but I don't remember as how any of the townfolk got shot, or even got shot at."

Brice surreptitiously threw a guarded flip of the head across the room at an impressive-looking man who stood in front of the sheriff's desk. "Don't seem to matter any to these folks, Marshal. See that tall drink of stump juice holdin' the beaver hat in his hand? One wearin' the black suit, sportin' the full white beard, and a waggin' his finger in the judge's face?"

"Can't hardly miss 'im."

"Well, he's been a doin' damned nigh all the talkin' ever since this dance started 'bout thirty minutes ago. Judge cain't hardly get in a word crooked."

Longarm squinted hard, then ran a finger back and forth under his mustache. "You know the man, Nate?"

"Oh, sure. Everyone in town knows 'im. Name's Buford Scott. He owns a drugstore right next door to the Equity Saloon. Biggest complainer and bellyache specialist in town. Constantly bitchin' about everything from pigs wallerin' around in the alleyways, to you name it. Seems to really have his drawers all bunched up in a knot."

"What's his specific problem today?"

"Well, from all I've heard, sounds like he mighta witnessed that shootin' you were involved in earlier. Think maybe he got selected by the rest of these folks to do all the serious jaw jackin' about it. They probably figured he was the only one who could match Judge Cain in a straight up nose-to-nose argument."

Longarm slapped Nate on the shoulder, nodded, then pushed his way through the jail's overcrowded office. As he got closer to Judge Cain and Buford Scott, he bumped into Chauncy Pedigrew. "What're you doin' here, Chauncy. Don't you have enough to do at the hotel?"

Pedigrew bobbed his head, snatched his hat off with both hands, and looked guilty. "Well, we're concerned down at the Exchange 'bout the recent shootin's, Marshal. Just cain't have this kinda stuff right out in our streets in broad daylight. Bad for business, you know."

A bubbling anger filtered into Longarm's voice. "Go on back to work, Chauncy. You've got no *business* here." He pushed his way around Pedigrew just in time to hear Buford Scott say, "Well, by God, this kinda behavior's gotta stop, and right goddamned now. You and your badge-totin', pistol-fightin' sons of bitches've got our women all agitated and excited. Cain't have it, I'm a tellin' you. Hell, my wife's so scared she won't even come outta the house. 'Fraid to let my kids even go out in the yard, much less come down to Main Street and visit me."

Cain cast a tortured glance over the tall man's shoulder and immediately spotted Longarm. A sneaky, relieved smile etched its way across his face, as he reached around his tormentor, grabbed the marshal by the upper arm, and dragged him into the conversation.

"Mr. Scott, let me introduce you to Deputy U.S. Marshal Custis Long, from Denver," Cain said. "Perhaps he'll be able to put some of your concerns to rest. Marshal Long, this gentleman is Mr. Buford Scott, owner of Scott's Drugstore."

Longarm shook the rugged man's beefy hand. "So

I've already heard, Judge. Pleased to meet you, sir. How can I be of assistance?"

Scott's fingers came away from the handshake and right up into Longarm's face. "You can put an immediate stop to all this promiscuous shootin' and killin' out on the streets of our town, right in front of businesses where everyone has to see. It's a God-sent wonderment some innocent hasn't already been killed in all the gunfire you boys have drawn over the last few days."

Longarm toed the floor, shook his head, and tried to look accommodating. "Hate that I'm the one forced to point this out for you, Mr. Scott, but the actions of blood-thirsty idiots like Selby Boggs aren't something that me, or any other law enforcement officer here, can control."

The crowded, stuffy room seemed to get smaller as other members of the self-appointed delegation edged closer to their discussion. Scott's ears and neck turned an even deeper red. "Me'n several of my regular customers witnessed that 'un you were involved in today. Seen the whole damned deadly jig. Think you coulda done somethin' other than shoot that poor man over a damned lazy-assed dog."

Longarm's eyes flashed thunder and lightning, as he came to full height and forcefully jabbed his finger into Scott's lapel like a sharpened stiletto. "Well, that just goes to show how little you know about such encounters, sir. Didn't shoot the murderous cocksucker over the dog. Shot him because he pulled a gun on me, and he would've killed me on the spot if I hadn't. As for that *poor man* blather of yours, think you should know a few things about ole Selby."

Buford Scott waved Longarm's yet-to-be-stated argument away with the hat he still held. "I don't give a bag of steamin' fresh horse shit about who he was, or anything he ever did 'fore he got to Tascosa. Rowdy as this town is, we've never had a middle of the day street killin' till now. Sure, cowboys do whoop, holler, and shoot off their guns now and again, but such boisterous behavior has to be expected from south Texas brush poppers who've been on the trail for over a month."

"Long as you're here, you're gonna listen to what I've got to say," Longarm growled. The smoldering lawman's knifelike finger got more insistent. The store owner frowned, rubbed the area of abuse, and took a step backward in an effort to get away from it. "Boggs was a killer for hire, Mr. Scott. He's murdered men, women, and children all over this part of the country—been in prison half-a-dozen times over the past decade, or so. Raped his way through almost every county in North Texas. He'd even made it all the way to the gallows twice, 'fore I ended his days on earth, only to be turned loose on a variety of technicalities found by a seemingly endless parade of scum-sucking lawyers and gutless Texas juries—a malady common to the citizenry of this state these days. But how the mangy, stink-sprayin' skunk has managed not to get himself hung is an abiding mystery to almost everyone in the western United States who carries a badge—including me."

Scott wagged his head back and forth, then swayed from foot to foot like a Baptist preacher at a tent revival about to deliver the true word of the living God. "Makes no difference. Makes not one goddamned iota of difference, far as anyone here is concerned. Can't have ambush shooting's after dark, or bloody, standup, gunfight killing's right out on our streets in broad daylight. Hell, all it woulda took is one stray bullet and any one of us here coulda died along with that Boggs feller."

Of a sudden, Judge Cain grew a new and stiffer backbone. "You're just going to have to deal with it, Mr. Scott. We've got a trial to put on starting tomorrow morning. The law enforcement officers I've secured for the protection of the court have my full faith and complete backing."

"You're backin' a man who pushed McCord and Boggs into a pistol duel neither one of them had a snowball's chance in hell of winnin'," Scott snarled.

Bolstered by Longarm's steely-eyed presence, Cain refused to back down. "I've already talked with a number of people who also witnessed the shooting, Mr. Scott. All of them, without exception, have told me that Marshal Long was forced into the unfortunate dispatching of Selby Boggs. So far as I'm concerned, that's the end of the conversation surrounding the incident."

Scott brought the hat up again and shook it in Judge Cain's face. "No, by God, that ain't the end of anything. Citizens of Tascosa didn't want Bronson Tull's trial in our town to start with. Didn't have any choice in the matter though. You politickin' sons of bitches from down in Amarillo didn't have guts enough to put him on trial down there, 'cause of his father. So you brung him up here."

"Now that's simply not true, Buford, and you know it," Cain groused.

"The hell you say. You're all afraid of Rufus and that sorry bunch he runs with down there in Amarillo. Now that old bastard and the worst of his personal brood is right here in our town, and we've had two shootings in as

148

many days. Hot lead a flyin' all over the place. 'Fore this mess is finally over an' done with, ain't no tellin' how many more people will die." A number of the other men in the milling group loudly seconded their leader's contention with shouts of encouragement and affirmative comments.

Longarm stepped between the angry businessman and Judge Cain. "That's enough, gents. This senseless argument is over. We're here to do a job, and it's gonna get done. So you might as well make up your minds to it. The law says Bronson Tull gets tried in Tascosa, and *that*, Mr. Scott, is the end of the discussion."

Buford Scott's head dropped. Scarlet-colored blood rushed up from his collar and reddened the part of his ruddy face not covered by a flowing, white beard. He stared at the floor for several seconds, then angrily stuffed his hat back on, turned on his heel, and bulled his way for the door. He threw an all-encompassing wave at the crowded room as he passed through the assembled congregation and said, "Come on fellers, ain't gonna git no satisfaction from these interloping bastards. Hell, they wouldn't care if'n we all got shot down in the street like them fellers this mornin'. Might as well be talkin' to the nearest herd of the U.S. cavalry's jackasses."

Longarm turned to Nate Brice. "Get Josh and Eli. We've got to see to it all these men make it out of the office and away from here as quickly as possible."

Judge Cain dragged a chair up to the desk and dropped into it as though bone tired. Longarm and the other deputies followed the grumbling crowd of angry townsmen outside. They stood on the jail's covered porch, or leaned against the pillars, and watched as the would-be mob seethed its way across the street, only to stop in front of the courthouse.

Longarm could still hear Buford Scott complaining, but couldn't make out exactly what was being said. It didn't matter. Way he had the situation figured, most of Scott's group weren't really out for trouble. They'd just gone along because someone else said they should and there wasn't anything else in particular to do at the time.

"Think this bunch might get itchy, hump up and do somethin' rash, Marshal?" Eli said.

Longarm lit a cheroot, then flipped the dead match into the street. "Doubt it, Eli. They've every right to be concerned. Hell, if this was my town I'd likely be just as pissed as Scott."

Longarm took a deep drag of his square-cut stogie, blew smoke into the air, then added, "Not to change the subject too much, but have you boys searched around the courthouse this afternoon?"

Nate shook his head. "Was on the way to do that when them folks showed up. We'll go do 'er right now, Marshal."

Longarm pointed with his cigar. "Head right for 'em, when you cross the street, Eli. Let's just see what happens. Bet they'll break up and hoof it for home." Then under his breath and to himself he added, "As a rule the average man doesn't want trouble, and when confronted with it, looks for the quickest way out. Bet Mr. Buford Scott and his *friends* ain't no exception."

Sure enough, as the brothers started for the courthouse, Scott's infernal gathering spotted the lawmen coming. The simmering group made a number of yelping sounds like coyotes surprised by larger animals and broke up their bellyaching prayer meeting mighty quick.

The agitated shadows of alarmed men darted among the scant trees, down the vacant thoroughfare toward

Main Street, or into various alleys along the way. Nothing like a show of force backed up with shotguns to get the attention of people who don't want trouble to start with, Longarm thought.

He leaned against the nearest porch pillar and smiled as the still angry, now flabbergasted, would-be mob scattered and heeled it in every direction to get away from the perceived threat. One of the Brice brothers laughed out loud before the three deputies rounded a corner of the county's newest stone edifice and then disappeared from view somewhere on the west side of the building.

About the time McMasters Street finally cleared, and an odd, uneasy silence settled over Tascosa's smoky rooftops, the thick layer of greasy, gun-metal gray clouds, hovering over the Oldham County Courthouse, abruptly split apart like a ripped saddle blanket. A pale, death's-head moon spread ghostly light over the harsh Texas landscape and, for a moment, Longarm would have sworn that heaven's skull-like mask flashed a menacing, toothless grin at him.

Pimply chicken flesh and an icy feeling of dark foreboding crept up the lawdog's spine as hc thumped the badly mangled cheroot stub into the street and stared into the empty eye sockets of God's spectacular lunar display. Somewhat ill at ease with such disquieting portents, he resettled the pistol belt stretched across his belly, gave the street one last, concentrated eyeballing, then turned on a booted heel and strode back into the jailhouse.

Chapter 15

Surrounded by the warmth, seeming safety, and real comfort of absentee sheriff Jim Best's office again, Longarm flopped into a leather-covered chair behind the enormous desk, pulled out a lower drawer, and propped his feet up. He'd barely managed to squirm his way into something like a comfortable position when the steel door that led to the cell block popped open. A short, thin, hatchet-faced man dressed in a wheat-colored linen suit, spotless white shirt, black string tie, and the Panama hat of a Mississippi riverboat gambler stepped into the room. He carried a bulging leather briefcase. The fancy satchel appeared to have been made from the hide of a sizable alligator.

"Sweet merciful Jesus," Longarm muttered to himself, as the antebellum vision of a high-bred cavalier approached.

The immaculately clean, shaved-pink vision placed his paper-stuffed bag on the desk. "No, suh," the vision drawled. "Cain't say as how ah'm that closely related to the sacredly divine, although ah must admit to sometimes havin' beatific thoughts now and again." The accent was as thick as syrup, and oozed with the soft, smooth-edged sounds characteristic of the old South. Images of magnolias draped with Spanish moss, and mint juleps swam across the backs of Longarm's tired eyes.

Sarcasm dripped from Judge Cain's lips when he noted aloud, "Actually, what we have here, Marshal, is none other than his *eminence*, Racehorse Alvin Parker. Mr. Parker is the esteemed and widely famed lawyer for that poor, unfortunate boy so cruelly incarcerated back yonder in one of Tascosa's cold, cold jail cells—which as you well know all bear a close resemblance to India's most infamous den of incarceration and pitiless death, the Black Hole of Calcutta." Almost as an afterthought, Cain added, "May God strike me dead if I've uttered one single word that could be misconstrued as hyperbole."

Parker shot Cain a devilishly mocking smile, through which he gritted a set of pearly-white teeth. "Why thank you, Henry. It's all just so verrah kind of you to take care of the essential pleasantries of crude introductions and such."

Then, like a carnival magician, the miniature man's nimble fingers produced a business card from thin air with a resounding snap. Accompanied by heel-clicking formality, and a flashy, insincere grin, the spotlessly clean attorney leaned forward and gingerly handed the card to Longarm. Parker's entire act was conducted as though making the presentation of something special, valuable, and much desired.

"Nice trick," Longarm said as he accepted the lawyer's card. "Beautiful piece of print work. Gold embossed. Right fancy stuff. Most impressive, Mr. Parker."

Parker's act continued. He toed at the floor like a self-conscious twelve-year-old caught milking the wrong cow, but immediately recovered. The uncomfortable smile vanished and was replaced by thin-lipped determination. "Ah trust, you've made plans to git my client and his dear, ole, white-haired, ailin' pappy who was recently ambushed right in front of this jail, from heah to the courthouse safely tomorrow mawnin', Marshal? Given all these shootin's of late, it would prove a terrible shame if'n some irate, or perhaps deranged, citizen blasted the bejabbers out of either of 'em on thair way across the street, don't you agree?"

Longarm glanced at the fancy script of the lawyer's calling card again, then dropped it on the desk. Parker smiled like a fox armed with a meat cleaver set loose in a hen house. As magically as the card had appeared, he produced a cigar the size of an ax handle from an inside coat pocket, but made no effort to light the beastly roll of maduro tobacco. Rather, Longarm noticed, the bantam-sized lawyer tended to use the gigantic smoke for little more than dramatic effect, or to punctuate his more emphatic remarks.

Judge Cain flashed a pleased smirk when Longarm shot back, "Well, now, I think your client is perfectly safe, Mr. Parker. Can't say as much for me, my deputies, or the judge, given that Bronson Tull's dear, sweet-natured, ole pappy is still runnin' loose somewhere in town—in spite of the fact that I've purged the area of a group of his armed and deadly henchmen this very afternoon."

"Oh, but you are grossly mistaken, suh. The estimable Mr. Rufus Tull is back yonder in the cell block with his sweet-natured, animal-lovin', Bible-readin', baby-kissin' son. Yes, indeedy. They're a perusin' the Good Book. Readin' the Sermon on the Mount, as I recall, and a prayin', you see. A prayin' for quick deliverance from this unfortunate mess we all now find ourselves confronted with."

Cain grunted something that sounded like, "Har-rumph, harrumph, harrumph," then said, "Told you didn't I, Marshal Long? Ole Rufus has no shame. He'll do any-thing to get his way, even if it means committing the blas-phemy of portraying himself as a Christian and a gentleman. Sweet sufferin' Jesus, wouldn't surprise me to find out that old bandit had recently fornicated with dev-ilish imps in order to get Bronson off."

Longarm pitched his hat onto the desk, then waved the judge into silence. He ran tired fingers through sweat-matted hair. To Tull's lawyer he said, "Well, I'm glad to hear all that, Mr. Parker. Near as I've been able to tell, both of 'em could use an extended dose of some kind of religion."

The lawyer rolled his icy-blue eyes toward heaven, stared at the ceiling for a moment, then locked Longarm in an intense, knifelike gaze. "But ah must also mention that he's verrah upset by the rude killin' of his good friend Mr. Selby Boggs. And the fact, as well, that you ran his other friends outta town without so much as a by yoah leave. He feels you've behaved most appallingly, suh."

Longarm glanced up at Parker as though examining a new form of hard-shelled dung beetle he'd just found rolling a ball of shit the size of a galvanized bucket around on the floor. Then he shot a guarded look at Judge Cain before saying, "Can you tell me something, Mr. Parker? Do you really think you can get Bronson Tull off for the killing he's been accused of?"

The nattily dressed, miniature attorney sliced off an invisible chunk of air with his cigar, then took a quick look toward heaven as though searching for indications of divine guidance located somewhere among the ex-posed ceiling rafters above his head. He assumed a deeply thoughtful air for a second, then grinned at Long-arm. "Why surely you jest, suh. Yourah talkin' to the best criminal defense lawyer in the great Lone Star State. Therah's no way in hell Bronson Tull will spend another day in cruel, cruel bondage once we present our case to a *Texican* jury and make the proper appeals to the reasoned judgment of twelve good and true men of character. This case is nothin' more than a steamin' bag of fresh horse shit, as farah as ah'm consoined, sur. And I'm absolutely certain a jury will find it just that way as well."

Longarm leaned back in his chair. "No doubt about it, Mr. Parker, you must have a lot of faith in Texas juries."

A cold, deadly, serpentlike look crept into Parker's glacial countenance. Behind an unctuous grin, he said, "Ah've nevah lost a case like this 'un before, Marshal. And ah do not intend on a losin' this 'un, eithur. Believe me when ah say, Texas juries nevah convict those who arah forced by harsh circumstances beyond any man's control to defend themselves unto death."

"You're actually gonna plead self-defense?"

"Why of course ah am. My God, Almighty, wherah would we be without self-defense as a legal method for protecting the rights of poor, innocent folk forced to dispatch would-be killers? Wherah would we be indeed? Good God, man, Texas would be nothin' more'n a dark and Godless place—kinda like Arkansas, as I have often envisioned it."

"Whadda you think about that, Judge?" Longarm asked.

Cain shook his head and stared at the toes of his boots. "Wish you wouldn't go maligning Arkansans, Racehorse. My mother's from Arkansas. There's not a finer woman on the face of the planet. Most beautiful place I've ever

157

seen is the area around Hot Springs. Gorgeous. Unlike Texas everything stays green almost all year 'round."

Parker flipped the cigar around like a conjurer's wand. "Sorry, Henry. Didn't mean to malign yorah hillbilly mama."

Cain's eyes snapped shut. Through gritted teeth he said, "As to those other things, Marshal Long. Unfortunately, and as you already well know, Mr. Parker is probably right about the plea, Texas juries, and everything else he just said."

Longarm kicked the desk drawer closed and abruptly sat up in his chair. "Then what in the hell are we all doin' here? Why'd I have to abandon a damned fine-lookin' woman, hop a train, and come out to the backside of nowhere? Sounds to me like the outcome of this fandango is little more than an empty formality. Why didn't you boys just turn him loose and get it over with back in Amarillo?"

Cain leapt to his feet, as though he'd just been challenged to a duel. "Because, by God, a reasoned and thoughtful grand jury, after due consideration of the available facts, rightly and justly brought a murder indictment against the son of a bitch." He swept his hat off, snatched a fresh handkerchief from his pocket, and wiped a flushed face. As he refolded the hanky, he said, "Now then, Marshal, I would greatly appreciate it if you'd run Mr. Parker and Rufus Tull out of the jail as soon as possible. I'd like to go to the safety of my cot back in the cell block and get some sleep. We've all had an extremely long day. Don't know about you, but I need at least some rest before tomorrow's fun and games."

Racehorse Parker hacked at Longarm with his cigar. "That there's another thang we need to cuss and discuss,

Marshal. It would be greatly appreciated, by all and sundry, if'n you'd keep these local interlopin' yahoos out of yorah cell block. I personally saw several of 'em a roamin' around back therah jus' befoah you came in this evenin'. God only knows what those hooligans might have done had you not showed up when you did."

"Who, by God?" Longarm shot back. "Who did you see in the cell block?"

Henry Cain's voice carried more than a bit of undisguised concern. "Yes, who?"

Parker appeared mildly shocked by the intensity of their inquiries. He turned his hands up in supplication before he whined, "Well, how should ah know? Ah'm a stranger in a strange land. Don't personally know any of these indigenous brush poppers just by seein' 'em. But let me think. Yes, now it all comes back to me. Ah remembuh Rufus a sayin' that one of 'em works down at that big hotel on Main Street. Has one of those really Southern-soundin' names. Right on the tip of my tongue. Cain't seem to spit it out."

"Are you talking about the Exchange?" Cain blurted.

Longarm sounded unbelieving, when he snapped, "Chauncy Pedigrew? Was that the name you're searchin' for?"

Parker's face lit up. "Ah do believe that was the name Rufus mentioned. Yes, as a matter of fact, I think he's the verrah one, Mr. Chauncy Pedigrew. Nice old Southern name. Thought as much from the verrah beginnin'. Surprised I had trouble rememberin' it. Anyway, you should tell the man to stay the hell out of the cell block when they's prisoners back therrah."

Cain stared at Longarm and blinked like he'd been slapped. "What in the wide, wide world do you think

Chauncy Pedigrew was doing in the cell block? He's got no business prowling around back there. Hell, none of that bunch of blowhards had any business snooping around in the cell block without our knowledge."

"Damned good questions, Judge," Longarm offered, then stood. "Might be a good idea if I go back there and take a look around. Can't be too safe, you know."

Parker smiled and poked at Longarm with the thick chunk of tobacco between his fingers. "My sentiments exactly, Marshal. Just cain't be safe enough in this day and age. Simply gettin' to the point where you cain't trust a soul. They's sneaky bastards on every turn in the vast road of life."

With Henry Cain and the still prattling Racehorse Parker in tow, Longarm strode to the empty cell where the judge planned to sleep. He went over every inch of the barred compartment, the bunk, even the floor under the bunk and washstand, but found nothing unusual.

After Parker got bored and ambled back to confer with his client, Longarm pulled Cain to the farthest corner of his blanket-curtained chamber. "Absolute stunner of a thought just came to me, Judge," he whispered. "What if those threatening notes you got didn't come from Rufus Tull? What if he isn't the man we need to be worried about?"

Deep furrows creased Henry Cain's brow. He scratched his chin, then rubbed the back of his neck, as though fist-sized knots had formed there. "Never even gave such a possibility a single thought—leastways not until now. Who else could it be? Rufus and his son are the only ones who have any skin in this particular game."

"Maybe the outcome of Bronson Tull's trial ain't the

game our anonymous threat's playing. Do you by any chance know Chauncy Pedigrew, Judge?"

The judge ran his fingers through thinning hair. "Why, no, I don't think we've ever met. Can't say as how I remember the man from—" Cain froze. For several seconds his unfinished thought drifted off into space without further comment. Of a sudden, he turned and, as though Longarm had ceased to exist, the preoccupied man set to blindly pacing up and down the length of the cell as though lost in deep thought.

"What? What did you remember just now?" Longarm reached out and touched the brooding judge's elbow when the man paced by.

Cain recoiled as though someone had slapped him in the face with the week-old corpse of a dead animal. He turned on the surprised lawman like a cornered rat. "Nothing. I didn't remember anything. Not a single damned thing. Don't know that man, Pedigrew, from a fresh-dug post hole, except in his position as desk clerk of the Exchange Hotel. Never seen him before . . ." His voice trailed off to a whisper before he recovered and snapped, "Now I must insist that you leave and let me get some much needed sleep, Marshal."

Longarm resisted as Cain pushed him toward the cell's open door. "Wait a minute, Judge. Don't you think we should talk this over a mite?"

"I'm sure this entire situation will work itself out in fine form. If the trial goes as I expect it will tomorrow, we could put this whole affair to rest pretty quickly. Then, thanks be to merciful God, we can both get back to our respective homes and sleep in our own beds."

From behind a suspicious gaze, Longarm said,

"You're absolutely certain there's nothing about Chauncy Pedigrew I should know?"

Cain pushed the surprised marshal over the threshold of the open cell door. "As I said before, I don't know the man. Now, please, run Rufus and that weasel lawyer of his worthless son's out of here so I can have a few much-needed hours of rest and peace."

Chapter 16

Rufus Tull dragged his wounded foot like it was killing him. The old man complained bitterly as he hobbled to the jail's front entrance. "Damn you, Long," he ranted. "Me'n Bronson was a conductin' a prayer meetin'. Hell, we wuz a readin' from the Good Book, and a praisin' Jesus. Don't see why I couldn'a stayed a while longer. Merciful heavens, the boy might get sentenced to hang by his neck until dead, dead, dead 'fore the week's out. 'Course I doubt such an outcome, but anythang's possible when it comes to a jury of weak-livered Texas citizens."

Longarm pulled the heavy front door open, got Tull by the elbow, and guided him onto the jail's rough plank porch. "Sorry, Rufus, but Judge Cain wants some privacy. Feels as how it's kinda hard to sleep when there's the rough equivalent of a tent revival goin' on in the cell two doors down. Have to say, I agree with him. Thought there for a spell you boys was gonna end up passin' the plate."

Tull sawed the air with a leather-bound, dog-eared Bible. He limped off the porch and stopped in McMasters Street, just at the edge of the weak, yellow lamplight spilling from inside the jail. "That's nothin' but another load of lawman's horseshit," he grumped over his shoulder. "You badge-totin' sons of bitches are out to see that my boy gets an opportunity to go a dancin' with the devil at the end of a piece of oiled Kentucky hemp. And I'm a thinkin' you just don't want me around while you're a plottin' and a plannin' his ultimate demise."

Racehorse Parker tried to pull Tull away, but the man jerked loose and twisted at the waist. He spit a jaw of chewed tobacco at Longarm's feet, snorted like an angry bull, then lurched into the deepening darkness.

Tull's dandified lawyer cast Longarm a snaky, satisfied grin, and once again attempted to assist the old coot's stiff-legged retreat. But Rufus still wasn't having any of it. He pushed Parker away and continued with his raucous, foaming-at-the-mouth, profane rant until the two of them had fought and stumbled too far away to be heard.

Eventually the pair rounded the corner near Scott's Drugstore and disappeared onto Main Street. Longarm was still watching their boisterous departure when the Brice brothers clomped back in from their courthouse patrol. All three men were laughing so hard they could barely contain themselves. Their infectious giddiness even brought a smile to Longarm's face, in spite of his ignorance of whatever it was they'd found so amusing.

"What's so rib-ticklin' funny, boys?" he finally asked.

Nate dropped a short-barreled shotgun on the desk and pushed a gray-felt hat to the back of his head with one finger. "Oh, nuthin' really, Marshal."

His less-than-satisfactory answer elicited another round of guffaws from Eli and Josh. Nate held up his hand as though in surrender, which only served to intensify his brothers' jocular response. "Now, come on, boys. Gotta let up on this," he said. "I done already laughed 'til my gut hurts somethin' fearsome. Y'all need to give 'er a rest."

Eli covered his mouth, bit a knuckle and made a futile attempt to get control of himself. Between trembling fingers, he said, "You're the one what done it, Nate." Then he bent over at the waist and burst out laughing again.

Josh Brice tottered away from the sport with a dismissive wave of the hand and headed for the cell block. Over his shoulder he offered, "Just gotta git away from you boys for a minute."

"Oh, now don't you dare abandon me," Nate called to his brother's back.

Josh stopped, turned, and leaned against the door frame. "If I stay, Marshal Long might learn some of your most closely held family secrets, Nate."

Nate assumed a fake, horrified look. "You wouldn't dare."

"Wouldn't I? Marshal, you know, me'n Eli done seen our brother pull some funny stuff over the years. Like that time he hit hisself in the head with a claw hammer when we was kids. God almighty, the boy bled like a slaughtered pig. Our maw thought he'd done went and cut his own head off. Me'n Eli laughed so hard we both puked out behind my paw's barn. Then there was the time he stepped on a tenpenny nail a stickin' outta that six-foot-long plank. Hopped all over the ranch with that big ole board attached to his blood-gushin' foot. Damn, now that was funny. But this 'un here done took the cake, I'm a thinkin'."

"Well, come on, now. Give it up, boys," Longarm said. "What the hell's goin' on?"

Eli ran a hand from forehead to chin, as though to wipe the laughter from a flushed face. "Well," he said, "it's like this, Marshal. We'd done gone and run off all them yahoos who stormed the jail and was camped out across the street. Done it exactly like you said we should. Worked out fine. Then we went a pokin' 'round the courthouse. You know, just a tryin' to make sure nothin' out of the way might be goin' on."

Longarm nodded. "Yep. That's exactly what I told you to do, as I remember."

"Exactly," Eli continued. "Anyway, Nate got to stumbling around in the dark and damned near stepped on Chauncy Pedigrew. Evidently, Chauncy was gettin' ready to squat and do some serious business. And, I just know you ain't gonna believe this, but Nate scared the man so bad Pedigrew went and shit hisself 'fore he could git his pants all the way down."

In spite of himself, Longarm grinned. "You don't mean it?"

"Oh, but I do. Smelled like a manure wagon in July. Man must have a rotten gut, or maybe somethin' died inside 'im. Well, whichever it might be, we got tickled, 'cause Josh allowed as how he'd heard of such all his life, but hadn't ever been witness to the real thing. You gotta admit, Marshal, it's pretty funny when you think about it. Full growed man a crappin' hisself like that."

Nate slapped his holster. "Wasn't my fault, and you boys know it. So dark over there, I almost stepped on the son of a bitch. Came nigh on to shootin' the poor man he surprised me so bad. Don't know who was most scared, though, me or Chauncy. But, by God I know who smelt the worst, once we'd all calmed down a bit. 'Course we've been hootin' and hollerin' ever since it happened and cain't seem to stop, 'cause of the way he waddled off a pullin' at the seat of his decomposin' pants."

They all went to laughing again, but sobered up when Longarm scratched his chin, then leaned over the desk and growled, "What, in the unnatural hell, was Chauncy Pedigrew doin' out there in the dark by the courthouse, boys? Any of you bother to ask 'im?"

Nate shook his head, then shot Josh and Eli a quick, nervous glance. "Well, he told us as how he was suddenly took ill from somethin' he et. Said he'd tried to make it to the outhouse over yonder behind Chilly Coombs's shack—that little adobe place right next to the courthouse on the west. But internal pressures built to the point where he just couldn't wait. Went to scramblin' around lookin' for a spot to do his business. Said he was in the process of squattin', when I ran right over him."

Longarm shook his head. "Did you believed that tale, Nate?"

"Saw no reason not to, Marshal. 'Specially after he went and messed in his pants the way he did, when I bumped into 'im. Damn, I almost felt sorry for the poor bastard, 'til Eli and Josh got to laughin' at 'im. No doubt about it he dropped one heck of a log that didn't have no place to go."

Longarm jabbed a finger at the deputy. "Want you and the others to go find ole Chauncy, Nate. Right now. Don't waste any time. Fine comb the whole damned town if you must, but find the weasel. Turn over every rock. Look in every closet of every house. Do whatever you have to do, but find the son of a bitch and drag his ass back here so we can question him more closely. You got that, son?"

Brice toed at the floor and looked embarrassed. "Well, yeah, sure, Marshal. Heard every word you said. But why? Why do we want him? What's the point?"

"Just do it, Nate. Right now. Get at it."

Brice and his now sober-faced brothers headed for the door. They hadn't been gone more than a few seconds when he stuck his head back inside and said, "You're wanted outside, Marshal."

"Now what?" Longarm mumbled to himself. He stuffed his hat on and trudged to the door. Lila Crabtree's enormous, six-hitch Concord sat in the middle of the street and was pointed south toward the Canadian River. A light flurry of snowflakes peppered Longarm's face when he stepped from the sparse shelter of the jail's shingle-roofed porch. As he approached the coach, a leather-curtained window nearest the rear boot opened and Lila's face ghostly white, tense, and almost moonlike appeared. She extended her arm and took his hand in hers.

Longarm removed his hat. "Thought you were gonna be here for at least several more days, and perhaps as much as a week, Lila. My goodness, girl, I was lookin' forward to an afternoon horseback jaunt, and maybe a picnic out on the plains before you had to leave. 'Course that was only if the weather held out."

"So was I, dear Custis. But the condition of my companions has grown worse—much worse, as a matter of pure fact. Especially that of my poor Mary. I fear they both might be suffering from some form of food poisoning—perhaps from bad meat they had in Dodge the day we left."

"Glad it didn't get to you, darlin'."

"Well, as you are surely aware, I eat very little in a difficult and continuing effort to maintain the figure that has made me wealthy. Wouldn't do for the infamous Naked Lady of the Plains to turn into a fat cow, would it?"

Even in the poor light he could detect the strain around her eyes and that further manifested itself in her voice.

168

"Feel privileged to say that I can personally attest to what a fine figure it is. One of the finest, in my opinion."

"You are the pinnacle of an extremely select few who can attest to such a thing, dear Custis." She leaned as far out the window as she could. "I had every intention of making sure you saw as much of my figure as possible over the next few days. Unfortunately, both of my closest and dearest friends are in dire need of medical attention that can only be obtained in Amarillo."

"Take it your wheelwright got back ahead of schedule?"

"Yes. He made the trip in record time, I'm told, and charged me plenty for that miracle. He was able—at some expense, I might add—to purchase a wheel to replace the damaged one. And, for an additional payment of course, our driver has agreed to take us the final thirty or so miles as quickly as possible. Normally I don't like to travel at night, but given the gravity of the situation, this time it cannot be avoided."

Longarm caressed Lila's face, then leaned forward and kissed her lightly on the lips. As he retreated, she drew her hand back inside the coach, then held it out again and placed the cameo and gold chain he'd first spotted around her neck when they met at the North Star Restaurant into his waiting fingers.

"My word, I can't accept such an extravagant gift, Lila. This bauble must have cost you a small fortune."

She closed her fingers around his. "Oh, but I insist, dear Custis. You can return it, when next we meet."

With her free hand, Lila Crabtree rapped on the roof of the coach. The driver slapped cold, stiff reins against his anxious team's backs and called out, "Rastus, Dave, Judy." Six massive animals strained against their heavy leather collars, and the Concord lurched forward.

Lila's fingers slipped from Longarm's grasp. She left him in the dark street alone, amidst a swirl of flying dust and nickel-sized snowflakes. For some minutes he stood without moving and could still hear the coach as it turned the corner onto Tascosa's Main Street, picked up speed at the driver's vocal urging, and then headed south toward the river.

Longarm ran his thumb over Lila's carved ivory likeness, then slipped the jewel and its necklace into his vest pocket. "Well, shit," he said to the icy wind that moaned around prickling ears, as he patted the bulge created by the stunning girl's jewelry. "On the whole, just seems like this entire dance coulda worked out a helluva lot better than it did."

Chapter 17

Chauncy Pedigrew squirmed in an uncomfortable wooden chair, then spit a bloody tooth onto the floor. He rubbed his swollen eye and tongued at the gap recently created by the missing incisor. "You boys didn't have to hit me so hard, or so many times," he bitterly grumbled, as though to himself.

Josh Brice gave Pedigrew a sharp slap across the shoulders. "You shouldna tried to run, Chauncy. For Christ's sake, we're all half your age. Man as old as you shoulda known you couldn't git away from us."

Eli, who'd taken a seat on the corner of the sheriff's desk, looked up from rolling a cigarette. "Yeah, and you shouldna fought us like you done. Woulda been a helluva lot easier on everbody if'n you'd a just come along peaceable, when we found you in your room at the Exchange a packin' up to skedaddle."

Longarm sat in the chair behind the desk, crossed his arms, then leaned on his elbows. "What were you doin' messin' around the courthouse tonight, Chauncy?"

Pedigrew looked sneaky. "Nothin'. Not a damned

171

thing. Even if I was doin' somethin', it's none of your concern. Every man's business is his own."

Longarm smacked the top of the desk with the palm of his hand. The violent and unexpected move blasted the sharp rap around the room like a pistol shot. Pedigrew snapped upright and almost fell out of his chair. "I don't have time to waste with you, Chauncy," Longarm growled. "Judge Cain's life has been threatened. I'm here to protect the man. Now, I'll ask you one more time. What were you doing behind the courthouse?"

Eli smacked the reluctant hotel clerk on the back of the head. "Answer the marshal, damn you."

With no warning whatsoever, Pedigrew's entire demeanor suddenly changed. His face took on an unexpected, angry, ferretlike aspect. "That cocksucker's name ain't Cain, and you cain't save him. He's a dead man. You can bet the ranch on it," he snarled. "By this time tomorrow he'll be deader'n Custer." Frothy, blood-tinted slobbers dribbled from between discolored, split lips. He wiped the crimson-flecked foam away with the back of a hand that sported cut, bruised knuckles.

Longarm flopped back in the chair as though he'd been slapped. "What the hell are you talkin' about, Chauncy? Whaddaya mean his name ain't Cain? Are you losin' your squirrely little mind, or somethin'?"

Pedigrew's head ratcheted back and forth on the bony stalk of his neck. He appeared to dread being heard. "The judge, you dumb bastard. His real name's Tucker Sweet. Captain Tucker Sweet, Grand Army of the Republic. Mass murderer. Killer of innocent men by the score."

Longarm's eyes narrowed. "What kind of horseshit are you tryin' to sell us?"

"That murderous bastard commanded a company of guards at Camp Douglas in Chicago during Mr. Lincoln's war on the South. Eighty Acres of Hell, that's what us Southern boys called it. I was a prisoner there for almost two ghastly years. Got caught on Missionary Ridge at Chattanooga. Sweet and his company of sons of bitches marched all new captives through the streets of Chicago to the prison like animals. Yankee civilian bastards all along the way spit on us, threw animal shit, yelled horrible things, even their damned red-eyed, screechin' women. Of the more'n two hundred men I arrived with, only a dozen survived."

Nate shook a finger at Pedigrew. "That don't mean a thing, Chauncy, and you know it. Lots of good men got took prisoner durin' the Great War."

Pedigrew's eyes glazed over with tears. "Hell, I know that. But by God, other men's past problems don't concern me one bit."

"How can you be sure Cain is this Sweet feller?" Nate asked.

"There ain't one shadow of doubt about it. Not in my mind, anyway. Recognized that evil son of a bitch last summer when I had to testify in a trial he presided over down in Amarillo. But, thanks be to Jesus, he didn't realize who I wuz. Figure he murdered so many their faces just all ran together. Stood in back of the courtroom after my testimony and swore I'd kill 'im."

Josh Brice said, "You're talkin' crazy, Chauncy."

Pedigrew's face was a mask of hatred when his split lip curled back over yellow-stained teeth. "By God, I saw that heartless bastard preside over the torture, starvation, and foul murder of hundreds of good men who didn't deserve such a sorry fate. Cocksucker'll sit at Satan's elbow when he's gone, and that'll be no later than tomorrow afternoon."

Over the next few hours, Pedigrew sat through an intense and sometimes brutally physical questioning. Judge Cain was rudely awakened by all the yelling during the interrogation, but steadfastly refused to even look at his belligerent, unrepentant accuser. He denied everything Pedigrew said, no matter how trivial, then flounced back to the privacy of his jail-cell cot.

Pedigrew watched Cain's retreat, then smiled through lips that dripped blood. "Don't matter none what that shit-eatin' dog says, or don't say. Like I told you before, he'll be dead and in a fiery hell shortly. There ain't nothin' any of you ignert fuckers can do to stop it."

Assuming that the hate-filled hotel clerk must surely have allies, Longarm shackled Pedigrew and handcuffed him to a chair. With help from the Brice brothers, he shuttered and barred all the jail's windows and doors, and made certain everyone was loaded for bear. No one got much sleep that tense night.

Bronson Tull's date with destiny dawned cold and dreary. Around ten o'clock Longarm had Josh Brice stay inside the jail and guard Pedigrew, while he and Josh's heavily armed brothers surrounded Cain, the Tulls, and Racehorse Parker in a human shield that bristled with shotguns, rifles, and pistols. As fast as it could be accomplished, given Rufus Tull's hobbling gait, they escorted everyone across McMasters Street, and hustled them into the crowded courtroom.

Longarm breathed a deep sigh of relief once the move had been accomplished, then posted Nate and Eli on either side of the judge's podium. He strode to the back of the courtroom and took up a conspicuous, clearly menacing position near the only entrance/exit, shotgun in hand, pistol on display for easy access. With shoulders propped against the wall, he listened with all the other attendees, as a fat-gutted bailiff called the court to order.

First jump out of the box, the jam-packed gathering heard a sad-faced prosecutor from Amarillo named Winslow Poteet rise and bitterly complain that all his prospective or legally subpoenaed witnesses had either vanished or now refused to appear and testify. Poteet finished by hanging his head and saying, "Therefore, Your Honor, the state finds that it cannot proceed."

A look of stunned disbelief swarmed over Cain's pinched face. For several seconds he appeared on the verge of a massive, quaking stroke.

Racehorse Parker leapt to his feet. "Your Honor, given the circumstances, as so concisely declared by the state's attorney, on behalf of my client, I hereby request a ruling for dismissal of all charges, forthwith, and his immediate release from bondage."

In spite of his obvious anger, the bug-eyed Henry Cain snapped, "Your request is granted, Mr. Parker. The prisoner is hereby discharged and is free to go about his business, but is advised that new indictments may be brought against him at a later date." Then, he rapped hell out of the top of the dais with a heavy wooden gavel.

An audible groan shot through a disappointed audience that had just witnessed what appeared destined to go down as the shortest trial in the entire history of Texas jurisprudence.

Rufus and Bronson Tull jumped from their chairs and tried to shake lawyer Racehorse Parker's hand at the same time. Angry, disappointed, pissed-off people poured into the center aisle, shook their heads, and grumped about the shitty outcome.

Longarm moved into the aisle and started toward the judge's bench just in time to glimpse a look of astonished horror as it swept over Henry Cain's face. The man's eyes bugged, and he yelped like a shot dog, threw his hands toward heaven, then fell over backward, and disappeared from sight behind the massive new podium. Those members of the jury who were seated closest to Cain leapt to their feet, then bolted from the box.

It appeared to Longarm that anyone left seated in the packed courtroom bounded for the center aisle at the same instant. A mass of shocked humanity blocked his view and progress, as he tried in vain to push his way forward. Before he'd made it halfway down the packed aisle, he heard Nate Brice scream, "Holy shit! Sweet bleedin' Christ!" Then two thunderous, concussive pistol blasts damn near deafened everyone in the packed, chaotic courtroom.

Panic and uncontrolled pandemonium set in on the already shocked and frenzied crowd. Women screamed and dropped to the floor. Some people crawled under the benches searching for whatever might be obtained in the way of perceived safety from a still unseen threat. Others covered their heads and fell to the floor. The most determined broke windows out and leapt through them, or fought and clawed like animals for any available exit.

After a prodigious expenditure of physical effort, Longarm forced his way through the seething tide of bodies and vaulted over a low fencelike affair erected between the screeching rabble and the court's official seating area. A thick curtain of spent, acrid-smelling black-powder smoke swirled around Judge Cain's elevated platform.

His shotgun fully cocked and at the ready, Longarm strode to Deputy Nate Brice's side. Appearing totally dispirited, Brice slouched against the wall and shook like a dead cottonwood leaf in a stiff wind. He pointed at the convulsing body of Henry Cain with his pistol. "Jesus, Marshal, look at that. Biggest diamondbacked rattlesnake I've ever seen. Got the judge right in the neck 'fore I could kill it. Damned thing is so thick, took two shots to blow it apart. Bet the poor man was dead first time his heart beat after the slitherin' beast bit him."

Cain lay sprawled on his back. Frozen in a strange, fright-induced pose, one leg tangled in the arm of his chair, the other bent and awkwardly twisted beneath him. A snake's head the size of a man's fist, and about a foot of the viper's still twitching body, was attached to the blank-eyed, shuddering man's neck—directly over the jugular vein. Near five feet of the rattler, as thick as a man's lower leg, squirmed and made jittering noises on the bare floor several feet away.

"We've gotta get that thing off him," Longarm shouted.

Nate waved at the horrific scene with his pistol again. "If you want to storm the gates of hell and bite Satan's horns off, I'll follow along and cover your back, Marshal. But don't ask me to mess with no fuckin' snakes. Been scrared of 'em ever since I was old enough to know better. I'll shoot 'em for you, but I ain't touchin' any of the slimy sons of bitches."

Longarm let the hammers down on his big popper, laid it aside, then knelt next the fallen judge. In a voice that sounded like it came from the bottom of a well, he said,

"He's still alive, Nate." Blank-eyed, and appearing numbed by the shocking events, Brice didn't respond.

When the full realization that he could expect no help from either of his deputies set in, Longarm steadied himself, then grabbed the partial snake directly behind its head and squeezed as hard as he could. After considerable effort, the rattler's powerful jaws finally flexed open. Fangs the size of thick straws backed out of Cain's neck and left a pair of ugly blood-engorged puncture wounds.

"Careful, Marshal," Eli called from a safe spot near the jury box. "Sometimes them slitherin' devils are just as lethal dead as alive."

Still on his knees, Longarm dropped the most poisonous segment of the reptile into one of several large, polished brass spittoons placed around the judge's platform. Then he motioned for the Brice brothers. "You've gotta help me, boys. Can't haul him by myself." Together they lifted Henry Cain's limp body, carried him through the near-devastated, now-empty courtroom and eventually back to the jail.

As the party of shocked lawmen struggled past the shackled and chained Chauncy Pedigrew's chair, then made for the cell block with their gruesome load, the battered hotel clerk burst out laughing. He regained his composure long enough to yell, "Told you, didn't I Marshal Long. Told you for damned sure. He's one dead son of a bitch now, ain't he? And even if he ain't, he'll be barkin' in hell soon enough, by God."

The rest of that day dragged by slower than smoke rising off a fresh cow patty in January. Longarm and his deputies did all they knew to do, but nothing really helped. When good dark came down like thunder, Henry

Cain was still alive—barely, but alive. Then, a little before nine o'clock that night, Josh Brice left his assigned post at the judge's bedside and strode directly to the coffeepot.

Bone-tired, Longarm wearily glanced up at his deputy as the man said, "Well, he's gone, Marshal." Josh took a sip from his steaming cup, then added, "Poor feller didn't stand a snowball's chance in Del Rio of survivin' a snake bite like that 'un. One horrible fuckin' way to die, if you ask me."

Nate mumbled, "God Almighty, when he swelled up, turned black from the neck down like one massive bruise, went to shakin' and a leakin' blood all over the place from his ears, eyes, nose, and such, sight came nigh to makin' me sicker'n a broke-dicked dog."

Chauncy Pedigrew, who'd been moved to the backmost cell, the very same cell that had recently been occupied by the now-free-as-a-bird Bronson Tull, cackled like a thing insane—and refused to stop.

Longarm slapped the desk top in disgust, rose, and wearily stomped his way outside to put some distance between himself and what he perceived as Pedigrew's growing madness. He slouched against a splinter-bristling porch pillar in the icy night air, pulled a nickel cheroot, fired it up with a sulfur match, and drew in a lungful of the harsh, deeply satisfying tobacco smoke.

A bleary-eyed glance toward the heavens revealed a jagged break in the thick cloud cover. The pale death's-head moon he'd seen the night before no longer filled the sky and stared vacant-eyed down on Tascosa. Instead, a full, blood-colored disk sent a prickly sensation up his arms and down a cold, sweaty spine.

To no one in particular he said aloud, "How the hell am I gonna explain this mess?"

●　　●　　●

Ten days later, Marshal Billy Vail tossed his favorite deputy marshal's handwritten description of Henry Cain's murder onto his beleaguered desk. He pinched the bridge of his nose, then gave his head a weary shake. "Altogether, Custis," Vail said, "I do believe that's the damndest report you've ever written, or that I've ever read in all my years of working in law enforcement."

Longarm stirred in the leather chair across from Vail. He picked at invisible lint on the hat in his lap, then said, "You shoulda been there, Billy. Honest to God, I personally believe the whole deal turned out worse than my poor efforts at written description can convey."

Vail massaged his temples as though he could feel an impending headache coming on. "Well, wish I could have been there. Would loved to have seen the contraption Pedigrew built that dropped that fuckin' snake into Judge Cain's lap."

"Trust me when I tell you, it was a well done piece of work. Near as we could figure, after extensive questioning of ole Chauncy, he'd been building the device for months. Son of a bitch bragged as how he'd started the job right after testifyin' at that trial where he recognized Cain, or Captain Tucker Sweet, whichever you choose to believe."

"Months, huh?"

"Yep. Got the thing installed in the Oldham County Courthouse a few nights before I made it to town. Honest to God, Billy, the finished mechanism was a near perfect duplicate of the entire top of the judge's podium. Soon as Cain whacked it with his gavel a spring-loaded trapdoor dropped open, slid that monster reptile directly into his lap, and a minute later he was as good as dead. Ole Chauncy said it took him two months of scroungin' under every rock, bush, and boulder around Tascosa to find the perfect snake. Said he didn't feed the creature the whole time he had it."

"And you never suspected him?"

"Nope. None of us did. Not until he got caught skulkin' around the courthouse in the dark the night before the trial started. Brice brothers beat the hell out of him, but to absolutely no avail. Don't think the man would've talked even if I'd of let them rip his fingers off with white-hot horseshoe tongs."

Vail scratched his nose, then grinned. "Seems like ole Chauncy did something of a Texas two-step on you and your boys, didn't he, Custis?"

Longarm's head snapped back in feigned disgust at the symbolic slap. "Yeah, well, I suppose you could say he danced around me pretty good. But hell, Billy, not even Judge Cain guessed the truth of the situation. He didn't recognize a man who testified in his own court as being someone he might need to fear. Had my own suspicions, but for the most part, just about everyone thought for sure all those written threats came directly from Rufus Tull. 'Course, if Nate and his brothers had happened along a bit earlier, they might have caught ole Chauncy leggin' his way through the courthouse window after goin' back for a final check on his snake-droppin' thinga-majig. Like everything else in this life, the whole affair all came down to a matter of seconds between catchin' a killer before the act, or failure. Unfortunately we failed this time around."

"Well, what's done's done. Can't call back the past. I am pleased that you took the time to escort Judge Cain's body back to Amarillo."

"Only seemed like the right and proper thing to do,

Billy. Suppose the worst part of the whole sow's nest was tryin' to tell his poor, hysterical wife what happened."

Vail stood and Longarm followed suit. The marshal placed a hand on his deputy's shoulder and eased him toward the office door. "We do what we can, Custis. Now, I suppose everyone'll have to wait for Pedigrew's trial to find out if he was telling the truth about Henry Cain not being the man he claimed he was."

Standing in the doorway, Longarm turned and faced his boss. "What if Pedigrew actually did tell us the truth, Billy? What if Henry Cain really was a murderous officer in charge of equally vicious guards in that hellhole, Camp Douglas?"

Vail pursed his lips, then struck a thoughtful pose. Seconds passed before he finally said, "Doubt it'll matter much. 'Cause, while Camp Douglas will no doubt go down as a gruesome chapter in the Union's history, murder's still murder, as you are well aware."

"Suppose so. But you know, the more I mulled the whole deal over on the train ride back from Tascosa, the more I came to understand Pedigrew's blind, bloodthirsty hatred for the man. Got to thinkin' as how I just might have done the same thing, if a horror story like ole Chauncy's had been my unfortunate burden to bear."

Vail slapped Longarm on the back. "Take a few days off, Custis. Hell, take a whole week. Don't let your mind dwell on it too much. There'll be another assignment along before you know it."

Longarm shoved his hat on, pushed it to a rakish angle with his finger, winked, then slowly ambled down the hallway. "I'm holdin' you to that, Billy—seven whole days off. Just like when the Lord created everything. No interruptions. No problems. But knowin' you the way I do, if you just have to find me, send someone over to the Holy Moses Saloon. Tell 'em to ask for Mike O'Hara at the bar. They can leave a message, and I'll get back to you."

Vail followed, stepped into the hallway, and watched as his favorite deputy stopped long enough to light a fresh cheroot. "Mean to tell me you're gonna spend a whole week in a saloon, Custis?"

"Adventurous lady of my acquaintance owns the place." Longarm threw his boss a mischievous glance, blew a smoke ring toward the ceiling, then said, "Last time we talked, she mentioned some mighty interestin' plans for any time off you were generous enough to let me have. And you know, Billy, whatever that gloriously beautiful gal has in mind, I wouldn't miss for all the un-found silver in Nevada. So don't send for me unless you have to. I plan on bein' mighty busy for a spell."

At the corner of Denver's Cherokee and Colfax Streets, Longarm stopped on the brown sandstone sidewalk and gazed up at the barely visible front range of the Rocky Mountains some fifteen miles away. Dark, heavy, threatening clouds obscured magnificent, rugged peaks normally visible to anyone who took the time to notice. Snowflakes the size of a man's thumb swirled around his exposed ears. He inhaled a deep, gratifying drag off the half finished cheroot that dangled from his lips, then slipped a note-sized piece of paper from an inside coat pocket. Only five words, in a carefully lettered script, appeared on the tiny missive. *We're waiting, Custis. Hurry. Cora.* He threw his head back, chuckled, shoved the note back into his pocket, and then heeled it for the waiting, carnal warmth of Cora Anne Fisher's room and bed at the Holy Moses Saloon.

Watch for

**LONGARM AND THE
HOLY SMOKES GANG**

the 340th novel in the exciting LONGARM
series from Jove

Coming in March!

LONGARM

GIANT-SIZED ADVENTURE FROM AVENGING ANGEL LONGARM.

LONGARM AND THE OUTLAW EMPRESS
0-515-14235-2

WHEN DEPUTY U.S. MARSHAL CUSTIS LONG STOPS
A STAGECOACH ROBBERY, HE TRACKS THE BANDITS
TO A TOWN CALLED ZAMORA. A HAVEN FOR
THE LAWLESS, IT'S RULED BY ONE OF THE MOST
POWERFUL, BRILLIANT, AND BEAUTIFUL WOMEN
IN THE WEST...A WOMAN WHOM LONGARM WILL
HAVE TO FACE, UP CLOSE AND PERSONAL.

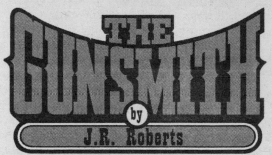